Dear S...

The Chapel of Eternal Love
Wedding Stories from Las Vegas

By Stephen Murray

Welcome to the Wonderful World of Love !

[signature]

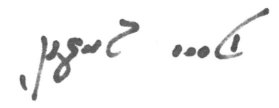

The Chapel of Eternal Love
Wedding Stories from Las Vegas

Copyright ©2013, Stephen Murray

ISBN: 978-0-9911940-0-1
$14.95US

Cover by: Cynthia Carbajal

www.thechapelofeternallove.com

Acknowledgments

To my family and friends—RJ, Sue, Grayham, Louise, Maria, Kolleen, Marlene, Suzanne, Averill, and George for all their support and encouragement.

To my writers group—Sue, Gail, Deborah, Nancy, and Donelle for all their invaluable advice and suggestions throughout the process.

To Brian Rouff and Imagine Communications of Henderson, Nevada for making this chapter in my life a reality.

Prologue

Las Vegas! The city that never sleeps ... the city where fortunes are won ... where fortunes are lost ... sin city. The glitzy, glamorous, entertainment capital of the world.

But there is another side to the city. Las Vegas boasts more churches for its size than any other city in the country. It is also home to an abundance of wedding chapels, earning its title as the "marriage capital of the world."

In the very heart of the city, one such wedding chapel opened its door more than fifty years ago ...

Chapter 1
A Tribute to Laura

Pastor Glen, as he was known to his parishioners back in a small community outside of Casper, Wyoming, was a man of very deep conviction and faith. A soft spoken, quiet man, whose serene and calm demeanor belied his tenacious and determined temperament. His father had been a minister of a Presbyterian church in Scotland before migrating to America shortly after World War II, and the apple did not fall far from the tree. Pastor Glen followed in his father's footsteps, with his equally devout wife, Laura, by his side. Laura was born in the rural community and had never ventured beyond Casper. She liked the quiet life and the security it offered. She was devoted to her husband and siblings as well as her childhood friends. They were her life.

In the early 1950s, Las Vegas, with its highly notorious reputation, had been infiltrated by many nefarious gangsters and the mob, with the malevolent Bugsy Siegel leading the pack. One fateful morning, Pastor Glen sensed a calling from his maker to head for the city that never sleeps to save the sinners from the evil that he believed to be so pervasive. Laura, ever the dutiful and adoring wife, stood resolutely by his side despite her misgivings. She was distraught to leave all that she knew and held dear, but was also wise enough to know that he needed her unquestioning faith and support. Within a matter of weeks they headed south for their new life in the Nevada desert.

Las Vegas was a far cry from the rustic, God-fearing community that had embraced him so readily when he first became pastor. Though he knew their faith would surely be tested, he was not prepared for such a drastic change and the transition was a tumultuous one. Laura had a particularly difficult time adapting to the colorful city that defied her conventions, standards, and values. In her home community, people helped their fellow man. She baked cookies and prepared food for those less fortunate. It was an honest, pure, and humble life. Las Vegas seemed to her to be a city full of swindlers, double dealers, and connivers—a magnet for shady characters. However, she and Glen worked steadfastly together as a team, as they had in the past, knowing that they were fulfilling what the Lord required of them.

After two years in their new location, Laura and her husband were elated; they were expecting their first child. The child would be a "gift from God" the pastor said, as he reveled in the idea of being a father. Laura took it all in stride, glowing as she anticipated the joys of motherhood.

Alas, it was not meant to be. Shortly before the baby was due, Laura was rushed to the hospital. There were complications with childbirth.

Pastor Glen begged and prayed that his wife would not suffer too much pain, and that his baby would be born healthy. His prayers went unanswered, as neither Laura nor the baby survived. Totally devastated, the pastor never fully recovered from the loss of his cherished one and the child he had looked forward to nurturing. For weeks and months, he agonized over his loss and begged for direction from his creator, repeatedly questioning his faith and mission in life.

His dreams were often invaded with the sights and sounds of his would-be child laughing and Laura rocking her child playfully in her arms, beaming all the while. He knew he would never find another Laura and his hopes of remarrying and fathering the children he so dearly wanted, vanished.

Yet for all the temptations in Las Vegas—the women, the drinking, the gambling—he always refrained. Providing food and shelter to the poor and offering comfort to those in need of his compassionate counsel kept him occupied as he prayed constantly for guidance. He remained disciplined throughout his anguish.

Out of the ashes of this tragedy grew a changed, stronger and wiser man. Through his sadness, he discovered the true depth of his love for Laura, and what a profound and omnipotent force the power of love could be.

As a symbol of his love and in memory of his wife, Pastor Glen resolved to build a small wedding chapel. It would be non-denominational; he would marry all who came before him in the name of love. He had seen photographs of his father's small church back in Scotland, and set about replicating the same gothic style. He decided to call it "The Chapel of Eternal Love."

With the relatively small amount of money from Laura's life insurance policy, he put every cent, and a considerable amount of his own time and labor, into the construction of the chapel. It was built using old granite stone. A solid oak front door with large, wrought iron knocker adorned the portal. Inside, five rows of pews, also carved out of oak, were assembled on either side of the center aisle, comfortably seating forty people. At the end of the chapel, he installed a large circular stained glass window. True, it was not the size and spectacle of the magnificent mosaic windows in the Notre Dame Cathedral in Paris, he thought, but it was very impressive nonetheless. He installed smaller mosaic-style stained glass windows at regular intervals along the side of the chapel. He deliberately decided on abstract mosaics in the windows as opposed to religious symbols. It was his desire that the chapel be open to all who wished to celebrate and exchange their vows of love, regardless of their religious persuasion or affiliations.

Below the main circular stained glass window, he ensured that there was an omnipresent large vase of red roses, when the season permitted, which always presented a forcible image to all who entered. They were Laura's favorite flowers. He endeavored to find other red flowers as a substitute during the winter months. A small piano was located in the corner, as an organ was too expensive. Opposite the piano on the other side of the aisle was a large, ornate display cupboard that housed assorted candles in varying pastel shades and sizes. He would use them in ceremonies if the occasion arose.

When the structure was complete, it was a fine and magnificent tribute for his wife. He had created an aura of tranquility, which he knew would have pleased her. He sensed she was beaming down from above with pride. Her loving, giving spirit and presence could be felt everywhere.

During the next few years Pastor Glen performed countless wedding ceremonies, but it was nigh impossible for him to reconcile the love he witnessed in the hearts and minds of those who came before him with the loneliness he felt inside.

They were constant reminders of the happiness he once shared with Laura. Despite his faith, there was an emptiness and hollow feeling inside his heart.

He sought and prayed for guidance about his future and where he could best serve the Lord's needs. After much deliberation and soul searching, he decided to return to his rural and bucolic life he knew and loved in Wyoming.

Over the next fifty years, the Chapel of Eternal Love encountered many changes of ownership. Yet people continued to flock to the chapel to get married. Oh, what stories its walls could tell if they could speak.

Now here it was, a new day dawning.

Rosemary, who had been the office administrator of the chapel for the last twenty years, was a warm, loving spinster in her mid-fifties. She was a gentle soul, with a slightly rounded face and a ruddy complexion, who wore her heart of gold on her sleeve. Always willing to go the extra mile to make the occasion memorable, Rosemary had learned to be non-judgmental, while witnessing parades of characters every day—and some were definitely considered questionable. Her instincts told her some of the couples' marriages wouldn't last, but it was not for her to judge.

She arrived early in the office every morning with Buster, her little dachshund, and immediately switched off the neon sign flashing "chapel closed." Having set the pot of coffee on to brew, Rosemary disappeared into the chapel itself to remove the dead leaves and petals from the roses—a tradition that had been maintained since its opening. She then returned to the office and played back the messages on the answering machine while waiting impatiently for the aroma of the coffee to reach its peak, at which point she could finally savor her first cup of the day. She followed this with checking how many bookings were scheduled for the day with little Buster nestled at her ankles, snuggled up. She always switched on the radio for soft background music to keep her company.

She donned her glasses, having retrieved them from her purse, and pulled from the little closet her knitting or her crossword puzzle—whichever she fancied—and set to work.

Another curious day in the life of a Las Vegas wedding chapel was about to unfold.

Chapter 2

For the Love of a Harley

Rosemary did not have to wait long for her first customers, even though the first scheduled booking was not until ten o'clock that morning. Startled by the sound of motorcycles revving up outside the office, she peered out the window at the cloud of dust they created as they spun around in the dirt. She arose from her seat and opened the front door to the office and welcomed them.

As was his custom, Buster lumbered down the couple of steps eager to sniff at the feet of the new arrivals, his tail wagging feverishly. Rosemary smiled. She always believed that dogs had an uncanny knack for intuition, and used the degree with which Buster wagged his tail as an indication of the love the soon-to-be newlyweds had for each other. Buster was like a weather barometer—always dependable.

Mattie and Garth clambered off their sparkling new Harley Davidsons simultaneously, and as the dust settled, Rosemary was able to obtain a vision of her first clients.

Garth sported a pair of faded blue denims with high-heeled leather cowboy boots. His black leather short-sleeved jacket was small enough for him to display his tattoo-filled torso and arms. Graying and straggly shoulder length hair hung from a red bandana circling his forehead.

"Howdy, Ma'am," he nodded to Rosemary, revealing his

deep southern accent, his smile exposing irregular teeth. He immediately removed a packet of Luckies from his pocket and lit the remainder of one of the cigarettes tucked inside.

Mattie was fully clad in denim and her auburn hair was cropped very short. Only just over five feet tall, she was considerably obese for her height. Although Rosemary observed no makeup, she thought Mattie's naturally rosy cherubic cheeks complemented her blue eyes, which gave her a certain prettiness.

As she looked at the Chapel of Eternal Love in front of her, Mattie wondered if she was in a parallel life. Marriage was never in her plans or her dreams. Born about an hour's drive from Biloxi, Mississippi, she was an only child raised on a small farm. As a child, Mattie was always considered a tomboy. Her mother was a timid, mousy, woman who was accustomed to being slapped and abused by her often drunk and abusive father. Mattie was only too aware that her father wished she had been a boy. She accompanied him on his many hunting and fishing ventures, which she enjoyed enormously, even though she was always afraid of him. Fortunately, she was a good shot and a competent angler, which pleased her dad and minimized his belittling diatribes. At school, she was shunned by most of her peers, having nothing in common with the young girls always mooning over the boys in the class, and not being welcomed by the boys who constantly shied away from any girl. Mattie became a loner, and because of her unhappy home life, lived for the day when she could leave and head for a life of her own.

During one of her early school vacations, she undertook a part time job at a nearby car and motorcycle mechanic shop answering the phones and ordering spare parts. It inspired her lifelong passion for motorcycles and her goal of owning a Harley Davidson became an obsession—her only dream. Each subsequent vacation she earnestly worked at the repair shop, stashing away a sizeable sum of money over the years, and as soon as she graduated high school, left her home for full time work in Biloxi. She did not even attend her school prom. She had never even dated, but she didn't care. Harley Davidsons were the love of her life, and one day she would own one.

Garth had not fared much better. Raised in several foster homes in and around Jackson, Mississippi, he was never able to bond with any of his foster parents or the other children who lived in the various homes. Garth, too, was a loner, preferring his own company to those of his schoolmates. They were all studious or athletic and he had no time for either. He developed a surly and taciturn temperament. By the time Garth was in his middle teens, and before he ran away from his last foster home, he had spent more than a few nights behind bars for various minor infractions with the law, though by no means was he a hardened criminal.

He did know his motorcycles, however, and was an expert at fixing any problem presented to him at the garage where he worked. It was a natural gift. He had established such a reputation and regular clientele that he opened his own repair shop. It was not in the best neighborhood, but the shop was his, and it became quite successful. He was his own boss, which suited him. He saved money with a steadfast fervor and finally purchased his own brand new Harley Davidson. It was his pride and joy.

Mattie had no social life of which to speak, and with

money and tips from bartending at night and what she earned from her job as a payroll clerk, she finally possessed the money for a sizeable down payment for her Harley. She was soon the proud owner of the latest model.

Coincidentally, Garth and Mattie had met at the local Harley Owners Group six months earlier, although they didn't actually connect for another three months when they each decided—independently—to journey across the southern states to California on their Harleys. Since they were both relative recluses, conversation was not easy for either of them outside of their passion for their bikes. They stiltedly discussed their separate plans, and over a couple of weeks, their individual journeys became a joint adventure. They were amazed at how much they actually had in common besides their mutual love of Harleys. Each had planned to avoid the big, alabaster cities wherever possible, as they both preferred mother nature's offerings of sleeping under the stars to cheap motels. Both liked simple fast food coffee shops to what they viewed as fancy dining. They considered anything beyond meat and potatoes a waste of money. They figured sharing the expenses would help them both immeasurably, and was a decisive factor in their uniting.

As the weeks went by, Mattie and Garth became excited with the common venture. For the first time in either of their lives, they felt that they had discovered in each other someone with whom they could relate and be understood. A bond of friendship was developing, although neither entertained the notion of something beyond that. It just did not enter their minds.

Neither Mattie nor Garth had ever traveled outside

of Mississippi, although both had seen much of their own home state. Finally, the day arrived; at sunrise—with great expectations—they headed toward Louisiana. They kept pace with each other, stopping periodically, but accomplished their goal of arriving just outside of Shreveport the same evening. Spontaneously, they took an unknown path off the main country road and parked their bikes by the river they happened upon. There was not a cloud in the sky as the sun set slowly, beckoning a full moon. They pulled the backpacks off their bikes and lay on their sleeping bags, looking up at the sky illuminated with stars. There was total stillness and quiet except for the babbling brook nearby, in which they had both bathed earlier.

Mattie and Garth felt at one with nature, and were beginning to feel like kindred spirits. They started talking openly to each other as they had done to no other their entire lives. Neither was judgmental and somehow they developed a mutual empathy for each others' troubled pasts. Mattie began to feel emotions inside that she had not felt or known her entire life. He was no dream catch, and he had led a troubled life, yet she felt at ease with him. They shared a mutual love of nature, hunting, and fishing, as well as their beloved Harleys. Garth was surprised and relieved that Mattie seemed to accept his prison record without criticism. He was even more surprised at himself for relaying personal experiences he had never been able to verbalize to anyone before. He thought that maybe he had finally found a buddy with whom he could relate.

So what if it was a girl? He didn't care. She had already made him realize how lonely he was. They talked openly until past midnight when, exhausted from the day's travel and their chatter, they fell asleep to the soft melodic sound of the stream.

The next morning they crossed through Texas toward Wichita Falls, struggling with their newly discovered emotions. The time on their bikes allowed them to analyze their emotions in solitude—their comfort zone. Even though Garth knew that Mattie was totally self sufficient and capable, he suddenly developed a very protective instinct toward her, and always kept her in view of his mirror while they traveled. This was not supposed to happen. He intended the trip to be carefree, and had planned his life to care for no one beyond himself.

Mattie started to see an attractive side to Garth, and began feeling a warmth and tenderness toward him that almost frightened her. He seemed to be a gentle and lost soul who touched her buried maternal instincts. She was thankful they had decided to make the trek together. As she rode with the warm breeze beating across her face, she enjoyed having him share her journey along the highways and byways. It was a happy time.

They arrived at a lake a few miles before arriving at Wichita Falls, and in keeping with their prior arrangement, agreed to camp again for the night rather than checking into a motel. They swam in the lake, laughing and splashing each other with reckless abandon, enjoying themselves like no time in their lives. Happiness was not an expression or feeling with which either of them was familiar.

They sat on the lush green grass for a while, before snuggling down in their sleeping blankets. With Garth's iPod quietly playing country and western, they enthused about their mutual observations of the sights of nature they had seen that day and charted their course for the following one.

The Chapel of Eternal Love

Over the next few days, they became more and more comfortable with each other and looked forward to nighttime, when they would lay in the quiet of the night and converse about the adventures of the day and the beautiful sights they had witnessed. The next day they headed to the Grand Canyon, eagerly anticipating the magnitude of their destination, and aware it was to be a highlight. When they finally arrived, they decided to make it a special occasion and indulge themselves by checking into one of the hotels within the park. They were not aware the hotels were solidly booked for months in advance, but the Gods must have been smiling. There was a last minute cancellation. They checked in and ventured round the southern rim, enjoying the breathtaking scenery and views, but more importantly, enjoying each other. They stopped at one of the vantage points at the Grand Canyon, just in time to experience the majesty of the canyon at sunset.

Capturing the mood of the moment, Garth turned to Mattie and blurted out somewhat awkwardly, "Will you marry me?"

Mattie smiled coyly as a wave of excitement overcame her. She hugged Garth as the tears strolled down her cheeks. They held each other, locked in a joyous embrace, feeling warmth and genuine love for the first time.

Back at the hotel, Garth stumbled across a flyer touting the Chapel of Eternal Love at the concierge desk and stuffed it in his pocket. No time like the present, he thought. They left the canyon early the next morning before the blistering sun ruined the day, and headed straight for Las Vegas.

Now standing in front of the chapel, Garth came and gently took Mattie's arm, kissed her on the cheek, and led her to the office. As they scribbled their signatures on the forms, Mattie wondered whether Garth had acted on impulse the previous night, and nervously inquired, "Are you sure you still want to do this?"

"Sure do, honey," he responded with confidence, joyously grinning all the while. "Never felt more sure of anything in my whole life," he added for good measure.

Rosemary pressed the button under her desk to alert the ordained minister to be in the chapel, and directed the couple to the chapel entrance. She was not aware of their circumstances, but she knew this was a marriage made in heaven, and would last.

As they scuffled arm in arm along the pathway toward the chapel, Garth flicked his Lucky to the ground and stomped the fire out of the stogie with the heel of his boots. Buster followed close behind, his tail still wagging feverishly.

The Chapel of Eternal Love

Chapter 3
The Twilight Years

Mattie and Garth revved up the engines of their Harleys and departed in a cloud of dust, just as a limousine pulled up at the Chapel of Eternal Love.

Through an open window, Sarah coughed and attempted to dispel the dust with a wave of her hand, fretting that it would dirty the pretty little frock she had purchased especially for the occasion, a pale violet sprinkled with small white flowers. A purple hat with a pale net veil covered her wispy white hair. With her other hand, she tenderly clutched a little spray of baby lavender colored roses and baby's breath. She was frail and petite but her well-lived face exuded a warmth and gentility.

Oscar emerged from his side of the limousine and walked round to open the door for his bride-to-be. He was tall and bronzed with a full head of thick, silver wavy hair that matched his trim silver moustache and bushy eyebrows. He was dressed neatly in a black suit; a lavender rose in his lapel matched those in Sarah's posy. Sporting a grey satin cummerbund and bow tie, he exuded a very debonair and commanding appearance. Sarah thought how handsome and distinguished he looked.

She stooped down to pat Buster who was sniffing her feet and wagging his tail furiously. He barked as if to offer his hearty congratulations. It was a happy bark.

Looking at the chapel, neither of them believed they would

be standing there about to embark on new lives at seventy-five-years of age.

Only a year before, Sarah bade farewell to her husband of fifty years. They had celebrated their golden wedding anniversary weeks earlier before he passed over into the next life. Childhood sweethearts growing up in rural Nevada, Rex was the only man she had ever known and loved. Rex was not overly ambitious, having served in local government all his life—not exactly making him a wildly successful entrepreneur.

But he was a success in Sarah's eyes. He was a faithful husband who, as regular as clockwork, returned from work at 5:15 p.m. every night. If he was late, it was only on the odd occasion when he stopped to purchase some flowers for her on his way home. Her birthday was never forgotten and he always honored her with a special event on their wedding anniversary. He surprised her with a cruise around the Hawaiian islands for their silver anniversary, and a Caribbean Islands cruise for their golden—the only times she had left mainland USA in her entire life.

Even though he did not possess the same devout Catholic faith that his wife held, Rex dutifully accompanied Sarah to church most Sundays. That was important to her and it made her happy. He was a doting father to their three children, taking an active interest in all their school affairs and achievements. He was a tower of strength and her entire life revolved around his happiness. Sarah worshiped her husband and could not have asked for a better partner in life. Rex may have been boring to many, but dependability, faithfulness, and being a good father were traits she admired and appreciated—and loved. She was devastated and inconsolable when he died.

Oscar's life had been far more adventurous. He was the star of his high school basketball team. With his dashingly handsome physique and rugged face he was never without a girlfriend. He was voted "most likely to succeed" and did not disappoint, having studied at Harvard on his multiple scholarships. Until his later years, Oscar had never experienced hardships. He learned to be an aggressive and cutthroat businessman and showed no mercy for those who did not conduct business in the same ruthless and competitive manner. There was no greater thrill for him than chopping down the competition. Mergers and takeovers were his world.

With his good looks and immense corporate power, he was an aphrodisiac for numerous females who seduced him without regard for his wife and family. Always willing to prove his sexual prowess, he was provided ample opportunity.

His faithful wife, Emily, was not oblivious to his many affairs and indiscretions, but always maintained her poise and dignity. She was the perfect lady and firmly but tactfully changed the subject whenever friends introduced into the conversation the subject of her husband's infidelities. She exuded class and was only too well aware that at the end of the day, he would always return home and that he would never leave her. She also knew, for all his philandering, the females were just pawns in a game to Oscar. She knew she was the only one he truly loved, the one he wanted hosting his large business dinner parties, accompanying him to many social events and for that, she always personified the ultimate elegant wife. She was content with that, and chose to focus her life on her children and grandchildren, her constant source of joy.

Oscar was highly successful at business, but he also

took some reckless gambles. His fortune waxed and waned numerous times over the years, and Emily was always at his side. Once retired, he still dabbled in the affairs of his multiple empires, even if the affairs of his playboy life were now a distant memory. The years had taken their toll, and he no longer relished the exciting world of high finance.

Sarah was relieved that Rex had provided for their burials many years before. It was typical of his attention to detail. On the day her husband was buried, Sarah and her children departed the cemetery unaware of the funeral cortege just arriving at a neighboring plot. She was too emotionally distraught.

Oscar had never imagined—even for a second—that his beloved Emily would predecease him. He was the one who lived on the edge, while she was strong, healthy, calm, and serene. She always seemed at peace. But there he was laying a large wreath at her tombstone, his heart full of remorse. He was wracked with guilt, regretting the wasted time on trivial dalliances. The one who truly cared and mattered was by his side no longer.

Sarah was at a loss as to know what to do with her life after Rex. He had been the center of her universe. How would she fill the lonely days and nights? Friends and family called offering comfort and extending invitations, but nothing helped fill her void. She started to visit the cemetery daily and sit on the bench across from her beloved Rex. It was the only place that provided her comfort. She talked to him, reminiscing

The Chapel of Eternal Love

over their life together, and kept the headstone clean and tidy, like she was still taking care of him. She took to bringing her lunch and spending most of the day there. It was peaceful and tranquil, and far better than sitting at her empty home. Most days were soothing, as she listened to the birds chirping and harmonizing in the trees and watched the branches blow softly in the breeze. Sometimes she felt Rex was speaking back to her and was warmed by his presence.

Oscar's mansion was even emptier. He particularly dreaded Sundays, the maid and cook's day off. He could hear a pin drop throughout the house, and the ghosts of Emily seemed to haunt the rooms. It became more of a mausoleum than a home. He especially missed those Sunday evenings when he and Emily were alone, and she made his favorite meal of spaghetti Bolognese with garlic bread. When Emily cooked, it was a home cooked, simple meal. The two enjoyed a bottle of wine as they sat around the kitchen counter, just the two of them. Aware of the adage that behind every successful man is a woman, he faced the stark realization that she was his strength, and how much he depended on her. Only too late did he discover her importance in his life and that he was really nothing without her.

He decided that, rather than remain in the household on Sundays, he would visit his wife in the cemetery. It could not be any worse than sitting in the vast emptiness of his home. For several weeks, he observed the frail lady sitting on the bench before finally approaching her and sitting alongside. They started small talk with each other. There was an immediate understanding of mutual grief and sorrow.

Their Sunday rendezvous became an anticipated event.

Having both lost their partners at the same time, only they could know how each other felt. For Sarah, it became the highlight of her week. They reveled in sharing their memories, photographs, and facets of their lives. When Oscar wanted Sarah to arrive earlier on Sunday so he could reminisce longer with her about Emily, Sarah explained she always attended church on Sunday, and could only come afterwards. It was at church, for some reason, she missed Rex the most.

After a couple of months, Oscar offered to pick up Sarah from her home, to accompany her to church, and take her back home after they had visited the cemetery. Sarah agreed, reciprocating his kindness by inviting him into her home on Sunday evenings and cooking his favorite spaghetti Bolognese, knowing that was the worst time for him. Besides, she was no slouch in the kitchen, as she had spent a lifetime cooking and baking. Italian cooking was second nature to her. She was apprehensive at first, knowing how modest her home had to be in contrast to his mansion. But her house was homely and full of love, and he appreciated the invites. The atmosphere was one of warmth and simple honesty.

Thus began a Sunday ritual that was never broken. Neither of them missed their Sunday date. They frequented the very occasional art exhibits together on other days when something was worthwhile, and took day trips into the country or to Mount Charleston every now and then. Slowly their hearts began to heal, and they enjoyed the time they spent together. But nothing could compensate for the loneliness when they returned home to their respective abodes.

Both were old enough and wise enough to realize they would never fall in love again. Once in a lifetime was enough for them. They were both too devoted to their deceased spouses—albeit in differing manners. But they also realized how much they could ease the pain of loneliness for each other, which became apparent the more time they spent in each other's company. Companionship was what they were both lacking, and what they had unintentionally found in each other. Sarah sensed a vulnerable individual whom she could look after in much the same way that she had taken care of Rex for all those years. In Sarah, Oscar discovered a woman who would provide warm and loving companionship in the same quiet and unobtrusive way that Emily had provided. She would be accepting and not demanding. Having their two lives join as one was a natural and obvious step for them both.

Their families and friends were skeptical, but ultimately gave their blessing to the union of this couple. Although the marriage lacked the passion of youth, it was filled with the deep genuine caring affection that had developed over the last twelve months. They had crossed paths with someone else with whom they could happily share their twilight years. They approached the Chapel of Eternal Love with no regrets and much gratitude, knowing that Emily and Rex would be beaming down from the clouds above.

Sensing how special the day was for both of them, Rosemary guided them into the chapel and started to watch the ceremony with joy in her heart as the minister declared, "Dearly Beloved …"

Hearing Buster barking from outside the chapel, Rosemary knew it was a sign of someone at the office. Surely it couldn't be the ten o'clock appointment. It was only just gone nine-thirty. She sensed it would be a full and busy day.

Chapter 4
Madam Emmy

Their ceremony over, Sarah and Oscar turned away from the small altar and headed for the front door of the chapel. Oscar gasped as he recognized the lady sitting in back row of the pews. Years in her profession dictated that Emmy never acknowledge any of her male clients in public, especially if he was accompanied by another woman. Embarrassed, Oscar looked down at his feet and walked awkwardly passed her. Sarah smiled innocently at Emmy, who nodded briefly back in return.

Emmy was the proud owner of the most exclusive and successful escort operation in Las Vegas.

Born into wealth and raised in the most select area of the Hamptons in New York, she was educated at the very best of private schools, attended finishing school in Switzerland, studied art at the Sorbonne in Paris, followed by a year at Amherst and a year at Wellesley.

Despite her decidedly privileged upbringing, Emmy did not care for the elitism that accompanied her family's lifestyle. She considered her parents' friends snobbish and boring and life in the Hamptons dull and suburban. Her mother and father were aloof, not demonstrably affectionate toward her. She never felt truly loved. Emmy craved excitement and a life full of adventure. She was determined, ambitious and committed to making it on her own with no assistance from her family. She needed to prove herself.

No city or place on earth had more appeal for Emmy than Las Vegas with its cosmopolitan flavor, its fast-paced lifestyle with people descending on it from all four corners of the globe. Being highly intellectual with varied and eclectic interests, she thrived on the diversity. In Las Vegas she would make it—and make it big. All the right ingredients were at her disposal.

Emmy was a stunning beauty with a mass of flaming red hair that she kept just below her shoulders. In fact, she was christened Ruby, because of the abundance of red hair that covered her tiny little head when she was born. Her piercing green eyes provided a sharp and alluring contrast to her hair and high protruding cheekbones added to her beauty, giving her a regal quality.

In order to meet the well connected, Emmy enlisted her services as hostess at the most prestigious Escort Agency in Las Vegas. She switched her name from Ruby to Emerald, a not-so-subtle method of accentuating the color of her eyes. To those who knew her well, she was called Emmy. In a short space of time she was meeting with the wealthiest and most cultured individuals on the planet. Numbered among her clients were international financiers, royalty, movie moguls, well-known musicians, artists, authors, playwrights, and politicians. Most were known by the public at large. Those who weren't tended to be high rollers at the casinos or professional baccarat players.

Most would be shocked if they knew what transpired in the penthouses of the various hotels and casinos she frequented. Emmy was a shrewd business woman with an innate ability for determining her own worth. The number of repeat clients and fees she received was an indication that she had what most men wanted. She also knew that despite widespread perceptions, it was not always sex her clients desired. Sometimes her clients just wanted companionship for dinner, someone with whom they could discuss a variety of subjects. It had been her experience that, contrary to public opinion, men were stimulated and aroused by women with independent and intelligent minds. Many, especially within the circles she was moving, appreciated the fine art of conversation. The clients, for the most part, were suave, debonair individuals.

One such client was named Dexter, who owned a range of quality jewelry stores in the major metropolitan cities throughout the globe including London, Paris, Rome, Tokyo, and New York. The first time she met Dexter, he was nervous and somewhat agitated. He was clearly a refined gentleman and impeccably groomed. She liked and appreciated that. As she sipped champagne, she realized that this was the first time he was seeing 'another woman' outside of his marriage. She attempted to put him at ease. Her experience had already taught her that men in this uncomfortable frame of mind normally just desired female companionship. She inquired about his family and hit the jackpot. He spoke endlessly about his three children and how proud he was of their accomplishments. He mentioned little of his wife, but clearly it was not a happy marriage. Emmy did not inquire. Not that she had the opportunity. The evening was more of a monologue as opposed to delightful conversation. It was the easiest money she made. All she had to do was be attentive—and attentive she was. She heard of his children's SAT scores, their sporting accomplishments, their hobbies, and school chums. By evening's end she felt like she knew all there was to his family—except his wife.

A few months later Dexter returned to Las Vegas and asked her to meet him again. He was impressed she remembered the names of his children. To her, she was just performing her job. Making the man she was with seem like the most important man in the world was integral to her vocation. It was what she did best. This visit, Dexter bought pictures of his children. He regretted his international travel took him away from them, and the apparent guilt of lengthy absences weighed heavily upon him. Emmy was pleased Dexter seemed more relaxed and at ease with her this time. The talk was more of a conversation as he inquired about her background and interests. He made it clear he could not, and would not, cheat on his wife, even though it was obvious his marriage was a loveless one. It was not in his persona. He was only staying in the marriage for the sake of the children. Emmy surmised it was probably also because of the fact that given his traveling lifestyle, his wife would surely obtain custody of the children, and would make it difficult for him to see them. She knew that would break his heart.

Dexter became one of Emmy's regulars, though it never moved beyond friendship. She was impressed that of all her clients, Dexter liked Emmy for just being Emmy. He loved being with her, and his visits to Vegas became more frequent and his time with her longer and longer. She loved the emerald earrings, brooches, and rings he gave her. *What woman wouldn't*, she thought. The key was he wanted so little in return. He had her on a pedestal and made her feel loved and wanted. Something she had never experienced her entire life.

Over time and unintentionally, Emmy broke the cardinal rule. She violated the unwritten taboo of falling in love with one of her clients. It was a career killer. She needed and wanted Dexter. Fortunately, Dexter felt the same way. She knew that nothing could come of it for another ten years, when his children were grown, but she was prepared to wait. He promised he would file for divorce the moment the youngest child turned eighteen.

Emmy knew she would need something to occupy her time and life in the ensuing years. Dexter wanted her to give up her life as an escort, but was emphatic that it was not a stipulation of their relationship and proposed marriage. It was the least she could do. She retired from being an escort and established her own agency. It was to become the most respected and exclusive agency in town. Emmy's ladies were the classiest, beautiful, most elegant available. She trained them well. Her ladies were all well educated. She insisted they become fully versed in sports, politics, art, culture, and finance. They needed to be familiar with international cuisine and connoisseurs of fine wines and certainly know how to select cigars for their male companions. Her clients, she reasoned, could visit any one of a number of establishments in Las Vegas if they just wanted a cheap thrill. When they came to Emmy, they desired and expected something and someone extraordinary.

She hired full time hairdressers, beauticians, and masseuses as essential staff who were available to her ladies any time day or night. She made sure her ladies were pampered.

Emmy was equally as demanding of her clients, and was in a position to call the shots. She ran background checks on all her clientele, established connections with premier escort agencies throughout the world, networking with them constantly. She was not adverse to turning clients away if they did not comport with her idea of a perfect gentleman.

She prided herself as now being 'off limits.' She often attended functions and banquets where many of her ladies were called upon to entertain groups of men during sporting or political conventions. But all knew she was not available. It gave her enormous pleasure to know she was still desirable, but unattainable. She had earned respect.

The years passed, and her agency gave her satisfaction, while Dexter passed on much of his duties to his loyal assistant. He spent more of his time in Las Vegas and finally gave Emmy the news she had waited years to hear. He was a divorced man and was free to marry. As she sat alone in the back pew of the chapel, she reflected on her past and how long she had waited for this moment.

Emmy was superstitious. Despite everything, she was a traditionalist at heart, and did not believe in the bride seeing the groom on the day of the wedding until they met at the altar. She arrived early at the Chapel of Eternal Love in a limousine, so as not to accidentally see Dexter. She tiptoed quietly into the chapel to watch the end of the marriage taking place in front of her. How was she to know that the groom in the ceremony was one of her former clients? *Small world*, she thought.

As she sat there in her green satin dress, accentuating her still stunning eyes, she toyed with the cluster of orchids of her bridal bouquet. Buster came and sat at her feet, looking up at her forlornly. She was too immersed in her thoughts to notice him. He slowly lay down at her feet, pining quietly.

She pulled the wedding vows from her purse that she and Dexter had written and revised many times over the months. She knew her part of the ceremony verbatim. Where was Dexter anyway? He was fifteen minutes late.

Inside the office, Rosemary knew something was amiss. Years of working behind the desk told her that Dexter was a no-show. She left her desk and walked through the lilac covered archway into the chapel and sat alongside Emmy.

Emmy reached for her Blackberry to call Dexter's cell phone. "This number is no longer in service," responded the automated monotone. Her heart pounded a little faster. She called the hotel, only to discover he had checked out the night before. She hesitated before calling his office and despite asking for Dexter, was connected to his assistant.

"I'm sorry," he said flatly. "I've been instructed not to put your calls through."

A knife went through her heart. She terminated the phone call and sat motionless. Rosemary put her arm around to offer comfort and solace. Emmy allowed herself a tear, and opened her green satin purse for a tissue. She dabbed her face. Buster arose and moved slowly and uneasily around the aisle. The pitter patter of his feet echoed through the quiet of the chapel. Emmy regained her composure, stood erect, and took a deep breath. She straightened her dress, remaining stoic.

Rosemary invited her back to the office for a cup of coffee and to tender some sympathy. Once inside the office, Emmy pulled her checkbook from her purse and inquired as to the fee. Rosemary chided her gently and instructed her to put her check away. She wouldn't dream of charging Emmy given the circumstances.

Emmy insisted.

"A contract is a contract. I am a woman of honor." She wrote the check, thanking Rosemary for her kindness. "There is one favor I would like to ask, though. I don't want to contact my limousine service. Could you please call a cab for me? As you can imagine, I hadn't planned on going home alone."

"Why don't you sit and wait a while, honey?" Rosemary offered.

Emmy shook her head, still fighting back the tears.

As Emmy pondered her future, Rosemary picked up the phone and dialed the cab company.

Chapter 5

Mazeltov!

The BMW followed the yellow taxicab into the driveway of the Chapel of Eternal Love.

"I can't believe it," exclaimed Giovanni. "There's Emmy," he commented to his fiancée, Becky. It was the first time Becky had ever seen Emmy, although she knew that Giovanni had worked for her full time as a hairdresser before he left to open his own salon three months earlier.

Giovanni ran from his car to embrace Emmy, kissing her on both cheeks, as most Europeans do—especially Italians.

"What are YOU doing here?" he asked in genuine surprise.

Good question. What am I doing here? She didn't know why Dexter had so abruptly left her standing at the altar. *Maybe he got cold feet. Maybe he reconciled with his ex-wife. Maybe his kids disapproved. Maybe he found another woman*, she mused. She would have a lifetime to ponder why. But she had learned to deftly divert conversation from probing questions over the years, and she certainly didn't wish to elaborate to Giovanni.

"Why I am here is not important," she said. "More important, what are *you* doing here? Let me meet the lucky bride." She feigned a happy smile as Becky climbed out of the passenger seat of the BMW.

Becky was struck by Emmy's beauty and elegance.

"But, Giovanni, I always thought you wanted a big wedding?" Emmy inquired lightheartedly, attempting to engage in small talk.

"Well, things don't always go to plan, you know what I mean?" Giovanni replied, slightly awkwardly.

Oh, do I ever. Emmy smiled weakly and noticed Becky's hands were empty.

"Where's your wedding bouquet?" she asked.

"Aw, shucks, I guess I forgot," Becky shrugged.

"All brides should have flowers on their wedding day," Emmy noted, handing Becky her orchids. Giovanni wondered why Emmy happened to be carrying them, but decided against inquiring. "You must come and dine with me after your honeymoon," Emmy invited, as she kissed them both before climbing into the back seat of the cab, extricating herself from a potentially embarrassing situation. "Shalom," she whispered and waved as the taxi pulled away from the car park.

"Are you sure you never had a relationship with her? She's gorgeous!" Becky chided Giovanni playfully. Luckily, jealousy was not in her personality.

Buster trotted slowly after the taxi to the edge of the driveway where it met the street. He knew that was his boundary. He whined softly, with his nose in the air, watching the taxi disappear into the distance. As soon as it was out of sight, he scampered back to the office to sniff at the feet of the newest arrivals.

Becky and Giovanni had a whirlwind romance. One Friday evening, Becky was closing the Kabbalah Center, which she managed. She eyed the man locking the door on the suite next door, where the "Giovanni's Hair Salon Opening

Soon" banner had been displayed in the window for ages. She wondered if it would ever happen.

Once the door locked, he looked across at her and smiled his big smile. His teeth were perfect, and his jet black wavy hair encompassing his tanned face with cleft chin created a stunning vision for Becky. It was more than she could stand. Extremely well groomed, he wore the latest Italian fashions; leather shoes and jacket and clearly custom-made tan slacks.

"Oy vey!" she mumbled, and her knees started to get wobbly. *Who is this Adonis and how am I going to catch him?* There she was, with a mop of ginger hair and freckles, looking more like an adult version of Little Orphan Annie than Little Orphan Annie herself. She didn't have much dress sense, and the only thing that actually matched was the color of her hair and her freckles. But Becky was a fun loving, free spirit who met life on her terms and no one else's. She was unconventional, spontaneous, an optimist, and saw everything through a prism of good-natured humor. Above all, she was herself. There was nothing pretentious about Becky. She had a heart full of love and affection, which she dispensed generously to all her family and friends. She was a true giver in life.

Giovanni walked toward her, extending his hand to introduce himself. *Don't faint*, Becky kept repeating to herself. She put her hand forward, which he took gently and kissed.

"My name is Giovanni, and I am the new owner of the salon next door, which is opening tomorrow." Becky's knees were getting weaker, and she thought they would turn to jelly.

"I'm Becky, and I … I run the Kabbalah Center," she stuttered. "I would love you to style my hair, I mean … tomorrow maybe, or the weekend, or next week, whenever," she babbled incessantly, like a stupid school girl on her first date.

Giovanni's hair styling schedule had been fully booked for weeks, but he could not resist the challenge of reshaping and restyling Becky's hair. He thought it looked like a hedgehog.

"I would be delighted to style your hair tomorrow morning. You can be my first client when I open the salon at nine o'clock." He had not intended to open until ten, but would take her in first.

"My God, he probably charges a fortune. I'll be paying this off for months." She panicked momentarily before considering the thrill of his masculine hands running through her hair.

As if he read her mind, Giovanni continued. "And since you will be my first client in my first wholly-owned salon, I insist it be on the house." Becky was sure he could hear her heart pounding and her knees knocking.

She was half an hour early for her appointment the next morning, hoping Giovanni had not forgotten. True to his word, she was in the seat at nine with Giovanni masterfully restyling her hair. He layered the frizzy tresses and created a fringe of wispy bangs across her forehead, with differing length ringlets down either side of her face. It was quite a transformation.

She had never fussed over her appearance, believing what was *inside* was more important than the *outside*, but the arrival of Giovanni on the scene and the proximity of their working environments changed her priorities drastically. When he removed the bib from her neck, and she saw the difference in her appearance, she leapt excitedly into his arms, thanking him profusely. He felt her warmth and sincerity. She handed him a little pendant with an amulet symbolizing good luck that she had brought over from the Kabbalah Center.

Touched by her thoughtfulness and generosity, Giovanni invited her to the official grand opening of his salon in two weeks time. Becky was elated, and asked her mother to make her a special dress, carefully omitting to tell her mother what the occasion was. Giovanni offered to style her hair the night before the grand opening. Her best friend gave her a manicure, but Becky demurred at the excessive makeup her friend was trying to layer on her face. "It's just not me," Becky said firmly. Besides, now that her hair was restyled, it somehow accentuated her freckles, making them attractive. No small feat, as Becky always considered them a permanent form of acne.

The grand opening was an outstanding success. Giovanni was understandably nervous, but Becky was there to calm his fears, provide him the warmth and encouragement he needed, and her sense of humor made him laugh and lightened his mood. Becky was already head over heels in love. Giovanni took a little longer, but the more he knew about his business neighbor, the more there was to learn. For all her kookiness, there was definitely a lot of depth to her. He admired her good natured and relaxed outlook on life, and her unwavering support and interest in him and his salon. He was fast coming to the realization that she would be the perfect mate and nuptials were in the making.

They decided to tell their parents on the same Friday evening, a happening that neither of them relished. After synagogue every Friday Becky always went to her parents for matzo ball soup and gefilte fish. It was Shabbat and a family tradition. Her parents, Esther & Jacob, were orthodox Jews who had been raised in Brooklyn. Esther was a seamstress and Jacob had spent a lifetime repairing clocks and watches. They had both worked hard. Their faith was everything.

The dinner table was laid out with the finest of tablecloths as befitting Shabbat. Jacob brought the braided challah bread to the dinner table for the blessing, as was their custom. Becky thought there was no time like the present and since there was no easy way to say it, she sprang the surprise announcement on her unsuspecting parents.

"I am going to marry Giovanni, an Italian immigrant," she stated in her typical non-committal manner.

"You want to marry WHAT?" Esther screamed. "You want to marry WHO? Is he Jewish?"

"He's Catholic, Ma." Becky nodded her head from side to side.

Jacob slumped in his chair. "Oy vey, my princess wants to marry a goy." He stared incredulously at the still unbroken bread.

"Not in my lifetime, you aren't marrying this boy," Esther said forcibly.

"I love him, Ma," Becky responded defiantly. She had always been strong willed.

"Oy vey, my princess wants to marry a goy," Jacob repeated.

"Enough already, Jacob. He probably doesn't even keep kosher," Esther scolded. "What would bobeshi say if she was alive?"

"Grandma would have understood, Ma," Becky replied.

Esther continued to fume. "After all I've done for you, Rebecca."

Becky rolled her eyes. The instant her mother called her

Rebecca, she knew it was time for the familiar guilt diatribe. She had heard it so many times over the years.

"When I think of all the dresses I sewed and the watches your papa repaired so you would have a nice Bat Mitzvah." *Here it comes*, Becky thought. "When I think of all the sacrifices we made so you could go to Israel on a Kibbutz. When I think of what we sacrificed to send you to Yeshiva University. And did we ever kvetch?"

"No, we never complained," Jacob interjected.

"No, we never kvetched. And this is how you repay us. What chutzpah! It's that Kabbalah! We knew nothing good would come of your working at the Kabbalah Center. I told you, Jacob," Esther continued, dismissing Jacob's tepid support.

"I am going to marry him, Ma, whether you approve or not."

"Then can't you at least wait until I am dead?" Esther retorted emphatically. She had never understood her daughter.

The seriousness of the situation suddenly hitting him like a thunderbolt, Jacob asked plaintively, "But princess, what about the children? What if you have children?"

Becky tenderly touched her father's arm. "Papa, both Giovanni and I are only children. We plan on having a large family, and the children will be raised in a house full of love. That's all that matters."

"That's all that matters to you? This is meshugge. It's crazy." Jacob stared at her in disbelief.

Esther fainted.

At the home of Gina and Mario, Giovanni was not faring any better. Like Becky, he always dined at his parents' house on Friday. His mother had made linguini every Friday night for as far back as he could remember. Gina and Mario were both devout Catholics, and each week Gina expressed her disapproval at the lax attitude of the church regarding eating meat on Friday. "The Pope needs to be more assertive on this," she proclaimed with regular monotony.

Giovanni broke the news to his parents: he intended to marry Becky from the Kabbalah Center. Gina and Mario knew instantly that she was not a good practicing Catholic girl.

"Mama Mia," Gina moaned, dropping her knife and fork and making the sign of the Cross.

"Mary, mother of God!" Mario exploded. "How dare you come here with this … this … this …" he blustered. The final words eluded him as he gesticulated wildly.

"Dad, I promise you and Mama will adore her when you meet her. I love her."

"And what will you say when you next go to confession? What are you going to tell our priest?"

Giovanni looked at his parents in disbelief. "I will say nothing to the priest about Becky, other than I love her. I thought you both would be happy for me. You are condemning Becky before you have even met her. I don't believe you are behaving like this." He threw his napkin down on the tablecloth in disgust.

"But what will the neighbors say? What will our friends think?" Gina reasoned sorrowfully, a tissue drying her eyes. Giovanni left in exasperation and called Becky.

"I thought my mother was going to plotz," she said. Giovanni laughed. He loved her Jewish expressions.

"What is plotz?" he asked.

"Oh, you know, collapse, have a cow," she said impishly. They giggled with each other, thankful that the ordeal was over. Becky always had a knack of cheering him up. They schmoozed for a while before hanging up.

The relationships between Becky and Giovanni and their respective parents remained distant and aloof. Clearly there was not going to be the large wedding that they both had dreamed of. They decided to marry at the Chapel of Eternal Love. As a last ditch attempt, both sets of parents were invited to Giovanni's home for dinner a week before the wedding in the hopes they would attend the ceremony and give their blessing.

The menu was planned to accommodate both families. Chopped chicken livers and Italian bruschetta for hors d'oeuvres. Gina and Mario insisted on bringing the salad, complete with Italian dressing, and Esther insisted on her home made matzo ball soup. Giovanni and Becky prepared meat knishes and Italian pasta for the main course. Becky made some rugelach using her mother's recipe, and Giovanni stopped at the Italian delicatessen for some of his mother's favorite gelato. They hoped this would show respect for both cultures and would meet with their approval.

Conversation was stilted, but the parents soon found common ground and wasted no time in trying to talk their children out of the marriage.

"I had always prayed that my son or grandson would become a priest," Gina wailed woefully to Esther. Esther shook her head from side to side.

"I just wanted my Becky to keep the faith. Follow tradition, you know?" Gina nodded sympathetically.

Becky and Giovanni were determined not to take the bait. The parents saw all the negatives and problems, while Becky and Giovanni saw only the positive possibilities and love and happiness. All four parents were united in their opposition and stubbornly refused to attend the wedding. Yet, in their heart of hearts, all four had to admit to themselves that what they saw were two people genuinely in love with each other.

As the parents departed, Becky and Giovanni watched them chat before embracing each other at the car. It was a start. Rosh Hashanah, Chanukah, and Christmas would be the next challenges.

Becky and Giovanni clasped each other's hands and walked to the chapel, deliriously happy, knowing that one day their parents would understand. As they stood at the altar, Buster nudged his way between them and planted his body firmly, looking up at them. They smiled at the dog as his tail wagged and looked back at each other.

"Mazeltov," grinned Giovanni.

"Ti amo," responded Becky adoringly.

Chapter 6
War and Peace

Kathleen's plane jetted across the skies. She would make it into Las Vegas airport and to the wedding chapel by the skin of her teeth, and should have known better than to book her flight from Minnesota through Chicago. Inclement weather delayed the first leg of her flight by four hours and then devastating thunderstorms delayed her flight from Chicago another six.

She had planned to arrive in Las Vegas the night before her wedding, meet up with Kurt, her husband to be, have a good night's sleep in her hotel, and be refreshed and prepared for her wedding at the chapel in the morning. Now all her plans had gone awry, and she probably wouldn't even have time to change before taking her place at the chapel altar. Still, she was pragmatic and decided to focus on the romance of it all. She was so exhausted she should have been sleeping as the plane crossed the states. But excitement precluded any form of relaxation.

Kathleen reflected upon the unlikely friendship and romance with her army officer flying in from war-torn Iraq. *Who would have believed it?* she mused as she considered the irony.

A graduate of Wellesley, Kathleen was a bright, articulate, and extremely competent attorney. Still in her early thirties, there was already discussion of her being made a junior partner. She was attractive without being a stunning beauty. Her pleasures were all things cultural, particularly enjoying lectures on a diverse range of subjects. They stimulated her, as did art galleries and theatre featuring new playwrights. She had a keen and active interest in politics and current affairs, which was her passion.

Kathleen was against the invasion of Iraq from the outset and campaigned actively against the United States' intervention, though she did not participate in protests or marches. That was not her style. She believed in the old adage that the pen is mightier than the sword. Writing letters was more her practice. She wrote to the president, to her senators, to her congressman, to the leaders of the Senate and the House. The chair and ranking member of the House Armed Services Committees were also recipients of her articulately penned missives. She kept track of the voting members and contacted all members of the House and Senate who were wavering in their support when it came to the funding of the war. She was resolute in her beliefs, and became more than a little frustrated when the responses she received were standard replies from staff. Probably some inexperienced intern, she always suspected.

To her it was not only absolute folly to invade a sovereign nation anywhere in the world, but unthinkable for anywhere in the Middle East. "Who appointed the United States the world's policeman?" she argued in her correspondence. This was all about oil and greed, pure and simple, in her opinion.

Her passion and wrath was heightened when her brother was killed while serving in Iraq, fighting in Kirkuk. Just over a year older than she, Brian was her only sibling. They had always been close, but became much closer after their parents were killed in a car accident five years earlier. Now she was alone. The intensity and frequency of her communications to the government escalated.

Kurt was under no illusions as to why the United States was embroiled in Iraq. It was clear as daylight to him from the beginning. A ruthless dictator known to have weapons of mass destruction had defied countless resolutions from the United Nations. Kurt enlisted as soon as troops were deployed to Iraq. No matter that the weapons were never found. He was still convinced they had been shipped to Syria, as surely all the world's greatest intelligence could not be wrong. Could they? He continued to reenlist for active duty to fight for the cause in which he so firmly believed.

Kurt was a handsome young man. He had acquitted himself well at school and college, enjoyed playing sports, and was an avid Dallas Cowboys fan. He had once considered a career in professional football, but acquiesced to his parents' wishes, being groomed to follow in his father's footsteps in the family run prestigious brokerage firm in Austin, Texas.

Kurt was in one of the first troops to arrive in Iraq, and was pleased to meet Brian from Minnesota who arrived the same day. They were assigned to the same platoon and soon became the best of buddies. Even though their backgrounds were different, they shared the same interests and the same values. They bonded immediately and learned to depend on each other more than either fully acknowledged. They shared any kind of food packages they received, read to each other any letter that came from either of their homes, and spent many hours discussing their own hopes and dreams.

Brian's letters from his sister, Kathleen, bore considerable criticisms of his actions. She disapproved strongly. He would never address her concerns when he wrote back, though, considering any attempt to change her opinion to be an exercise in futility. As Brian recited from her letters, Kurt listened to Kathleen's rants, and tried to see things from her perspective. He admired her intensity, even though he disagreed with her.

Kurt, too, was devastated when Brian was killed. They had endured much together. The horrors of war they witnessed were life-altering experiences for both. He recalled the anguish they both felt the first time they killed in battle, as well as the joys when they rescued and saved a child's life. Kurt felt an emptiness when Brian was killed.

After Brian's death, Kurt sat alone and penned a letter to Kathleen expressing his condolences, explaining how much her brother had meant to him. He ripped up several attempts in the process, before settling upon one that conveyed his sentiments accurately. He tried to reassure Kathleen that Brian had died for a noble and worthy cause.

"Noble cause, indeed!" Kathleen fumed to herself as she read the letter. She fired back a response stating that in her opinion the cause was neither. Somewhat offended, Kurt took it upon himself to reply, indicating the positive differences their presence had made, describing in depth his and Brian's observations on the day of the first Iraqi election and how truly inspiring it had been.

The Chapel of Eternal Love

Kathleen was surprised to receive Kurt's second letter. She did not expect to hear from him, once his obligatory sympathy letter had been written. She felt a little remorseful over the stern manner in which she had originally responded, and wrote a letter of apology for the harsh tone in her first communication. After all, Kurt didn't have to write to her. She conceded Kurt's point about the election, but it did not change her fundamental opinion.

When her second letter arrived, Kurt ripped it open. He knew from her prior correspondence with Brian how unrelenting she was in her opinions, but he respected her well-reasoned arguments and the way she championed her views persuasively in her letters to the government officials. She had even given him cause to rethink some of his thoughts on the subject, which he had once considered unshakeable. He accepted her apology, and responded with a letter including some photographs of himself and Brian holding Iraqi babies and standing outside the newly built schools and hospitals. He tried to convey some of the more humanitarian events he was witnessing, which, in his view, justified their mission.

Kathleen was grateful for his letters and photos. She could feel her brother's presence through Kurt's letters, as if Brian was still alive. Some of the phrases and expressions Kurt used were phrases Brian would have used. But Brian had failed to inform her of just how handsome his best buddy was. The pictures he sent really touched her heartstrings. She appreciated Kurt's anecdotes, which Brian had often refrained from in his letters. Her brother tended to inquire as to their friends' well being and what his baby sister was doing. Knowing how she felt, he kept events in Iraq out of his correspondence as much as possible. Kurt's letters gave her more of an insight into what was actually happening on the ground, on a day-to-day basis, offering her a different perspective.

The correspondence between Kathleen and Kurt increased, though it was difficult. Computer access and emails were nonexistent where he was stationed. Delivery of regular mail in Iraq was erratic; Kurt often received three letters on one day and then nothing for a week. He tried to write to Kathleen at least every other day before he went to sleep, describing the horrors and the triumphs he was witnessing. He appreciated the female companionship that Kathleen offered. His girlfriend back home ended their relationship shortly after he arrived in Iraq and had married one of his closest friends, and he had only brothers—three of them—back home. He especially liked her scented envelopes.

As time went by, Kurt was drawn to this fiery lady and her passionate intensity, the younger sister of his best buddy. The letters began taking on more than a platonic tone. He was beginning to think that maybe she was right all along. Maybe things could have, or should have, been handled differently, and if they had, maybe there would have been fewer casualties. Kathleen also surprised herself by conceding, albeit grudgingly, that maybe Kurt did have some valid points. Clearly the people of Iraq were better off than they had been for years. Maybe children and women did stand to gain a better life. She still could not conclude that the end justified the means, but she was willing to accept the cause may have been noble.

She was even more surprised when Kurt wrote one day asking for her hand in marriage, and she responded yes. Their correspondence had endured for nearly five years, and had softened with the passage of time. They started making plans for fulfilling their hopes and dreams and their letters became more an exchange of optimistic visions for their future and less about a global situation that, try as they might as two specks in the universe, neither would be able to alter in any meaningful way, despite their valiant efforts.

Finally, Kurt was granted one week's leave. He wanted to have his wedding and honeymoon in fun-loving Las Vegas, which made perfect sense. Given the fact that it would take him a day to fly there and a day to return to Iraq, they would only have four short days together. Kathleen did not have any notions of a grand white wedding. The simple, sensible, no-fuss approach was more to her tastes. The situation in and of itself was romantic enough for her. It was not as if she had a father, or even a brother now, to walk her down the aisle. Kathleen located the wedding chapel and made all the necessary plans, such as they were. It was far more practical for her to arrange than for Kurt to initiate in far off Iraq.

By the time her plane touched down at McCarran International Airport, she had less than half an hour before her wedding. As she caught the tram across the airport, she called the chapel to see if Kurt had arrived and to explain she might be a little late. Rosemary was very calm and reassuring, advising Kathleen that there would be a place for her to change into her wedding dress and not to worry. Everything would be just fine.

Kathleen hurried out to a long line of passengers waiting

for cabs. She was desperate, but once he was aware of her predicament, a kind angel dressed in a military uniform forfeited his place at the front of the line. He understood. She was on her way; her heart now racing.

As the cab entered the driveway to the chapel, she saw her handsome, and soon-to-be husband, standing at the entrance to the chapel, fully resplendent in his army uniform with all his decorations. She ducked in the cab so that he wouldn't see her and she could slip quietly into the office unnoticed. She didn't want Kurt's first view of her to be with disheveled hair, and creased winter clothes.

Rosemary ushered her to the back room and helped her change into her cream colored, stylish, satin knee length dress, and a small matching brocade hat with a diaphanous veil. Rosemary had already been into the chapel and snipped off a couple of roses from the ever-present floral arrangement, knowing full well that Kathleen would not have any time to obtain a bouquet. She thought it more appropriate than the small ready-made bouquets that were sold in the office. Kathleen applied her makeup as quickly as she could, while Rosemary fluffed and sprayed her hair. She was used to helping out in last minute situations. Kathleen hugged Rosemary, expressing her gratitude.

Kathleen took a deep breath, calmed herself, and walked quickly to the chapel to meet her Kurt. Just before she arrived at the door, she realized that she had forgotten something in her luggage. She hurriedly returned to the office, opened her suitcase, and retrieved two large framed photographs. One was a photo of her and Brian before he went to Iraq, and the other, of Brian and Kurt outside a school in Kirkuk. She intended to place them on either side of the altar, wanting Brian to be the witness to their nuptials. She was confident she had Brian's blessing and knew they would feel his presence. She felt his being and knew he was smiling at the unfolding of events.

Both Kurt and Kathleen were a little nervous now. It had been at the back of both of their minds that if they had met the evening before, as originally planned, and the attraction was not there, they would just make the most of a fun weekend in sin city. That was no longer an option, and now it was all or nothing. They need not have worried, though, as their fears were immediately alleviated when they first cast their eyes on each other and felt each other's touch.

Kurt was stunned when Kathleen appeared in front of him. She looked like a goddess, and was much more beautiful in person than her photographs had portrayed. Kurt was exactly as Kathleen had pictured. As they locked in each other's arms, they knew their marriage was destined to be. The warmth, love, and tenderness that had been building over the last five years was finally able to be physically expressed.

After their passionate and frantic embrace at the chapel's entrance, the two walked arm in arm down the short aisle to the altar with tears of happiness flowing down Kathleen's cheeks. Buster, recognizing a military uniform, and sensing the solemnity of the occasion, sat down next to Kurt, front paws and legs upright, nose in the air, his tail firmly outstretched, bathing in the radiance of the deliriously happy couple.

Love had indeed conquered all.

Chapter 7

A Marriage of Convenience

Buster growled nervously from the steps of the office, and the hair stiffened on his back as he watched Jake slouching along the driveway heading toward him. Rosemary peered out the window to see who was giving her pet so much consternation. She always felt uncomfortable when Buster barked or growled.

Jake was dressed in casual denims and sneakers and sporting a tee-shirt with a skull and crossbones on the front. *Not exactly a dream catch*, she thought as she observed him scuffing his way to the office door, hands in his pockets. She pondered the set of circumstances that bought him and his future wife to the chapel. And where was she?

As if reading her mind, he asked gruffly, "Rosa here yet?" Rosemary suggested that he check inside the chapel and wait for her there in the event she hadn't arrived yet. Buster was now barking furiously and ferociously, parked protectively in front of Rosemary.

Jake turned and headed toward the chapel. A few moments later Rosemary observed a slim, attractive young lady in a rather plain pant suit enter the chapel. Rosa had arrived.

Rosa was a very pretty young female in her early twenties. Her trim figure belied the fact that she was the mother of four young children. Her long flowing black hair and olive complexion advertised her Latin American background. She had travelled to America from Puerto San Jose in Guatemala. It had not been an easy journey making her way through Mexico and paying for herself to be smuggled into the United States, but she was determined to do what was necessary. She worshipped her husband, who was in need of eye surgery, an operation that was only possible in the United States. The only way they could ever afford the operation was for Rosa to come to America to work. Streets in America were paved with gold, they both thought. It was heart-wrenching to leave behind her husband and four *ninos*, but she knew it was for all the right reasons.

Rosa steered clear of the Arizona and California border towns and headed toward Las Vegas. She knew it would be easy to live in the shadows of a city with such a transient population. Alas, her dreams of making a fortune quickly eroded, as she discovered it was not easy to obtain work without all the required documentation. She was finally hired as a cleaner at a seedy and sleazy motel off the strip in the downtown part of Las Vegas, where the rooms were rented by the hour. The hotel manager asked her no questions and always paid her cash. She knew he was taking advantage of her by being paid a meager four dollars an hour, way below the legal minimum wage, but she had no bargaining chips. The manager, without asking, knew of her circumstances. He had hired countless of her type before. He knew how to work the system.

Rosa hated her job. The dingy rooms, with faded wallpaper and cigarette-burned carpets, reeked of stale smoke and booze and were always in such a mess when she went to change the sheets and clean the bathrooms. She worked six days a week for ten hours a day, alternating day and night shifts with Carmen, with whom she shared a studio apartment. It kept her costs to a minimum, so she could send much of her hard-earned money to the family each week, hoping they would be saving it for the surgery. On Sundays, Rosa always went to church, while Carmen had a private cleaning job at the home of a wealthy and prominent attorney. Carmen always returned with eighty dollars cash after only five hours work. That was double her regular job and for half the number of hours. Rosa wished she could obtain a Sunday job and envied Carmen, as the extra money would help tremendously.

Rosa and Carmen had been settled in their routine for almost a year, when late one Friday night, Rosa returned home and was horrified to discover the Immigration and Naturalization Department had raided their apartment building. Carmen was one of the people who had been arrested and taken off to who knows where. Rosa panicked. She couldn't be arrested or deported. What if she was thrown in jail? How could she afford her apartment without Carmen? She couldn't lose her job. She was at a loss as to what to do. She was frantic and struggled to keep calm, barely sleeping that night, locking herself into the apartment and ignoring all the outside noise, chatter, and confusion.

She woke the next morning and, for once, was thankful to be going to work; somehow the motel seemed safe and secure. As she was leaving, she noticed a note had been pushed under the apartment door. She scooped it up and read, "Call Jake at 7:00 p.m. if you need help." It listed a phone number. She was nervous and fearful. Was it a trap? She worried all day long, while considering her limited options. There really were none.

With much trepidation she called Jake at the appointed time.

"Meet me at Manuel's Tacos in five minutes," he said. "I will be wearing a tee-shirt with a skull and crossbones on the front," and hung up from the public phone booth on the street corner. Rosa was relieved that Manuel's was just along the street and was a popular diner. She would be meeting Jake in the open and nothing could happen to her. She hurried along, wrapping a shawl around her shoulders.

Jake was not one to mince words. "I marry you. You become a legal citizen. You don't have to worry about being arrested or deported ever again. I know you're illegal. I used to date Carmen. She told me about you. Cost you just three thousand dollars." He knew Rosa was desperate.

"Three thousand dollars?" Rosa screamed in disbelief. She would not make that in a lifetime.

Jake shrugged. "Take it or leave it. You have twenty-four hours. I will call you at seven tomorrow evening." With that, he left.

Rosa knew she had no choice, but how would she raise the extra money? Suddenly, she had a flash of inspiration. Knowing where Carmen's attorney client lived, and aware they would be expecting Carmen the next day, she decided to substitute Carmen's presence with her own, explaining Carmen's absence away. At eighty dollars a week, she would only have to work for nine months to accumulate the three thousand dollars. It was worth it.

She woke Sunday morning and travelled the two necessary bus rides to the home of Al and Elizabeth Baines. She stood nervously as she rang the doorbell. Rosa was relieved when Elizabeth answered the door, happy to see the warm smile on the other side of the doorframe. Carmen had told her how sweet, kind, and generous Elizabeth was. She was careful not to explain the truth behind Carmen's absence and relayed that family health issues required Carmen to return to her native El Salvador. Rosa offered to do the cleaning in the interim. Elizabeth was very grateful and thanked Rosa profusely for being so considerate. Rosa made sure she did an outstanding job, so she would be given the opportunity to return the next week. At the end of her work schedule that morning, Elizabeth ushered her into the office where Al was at work. Al eyed Rosa up and down. Clearly he had a roving eye. "My husband always takes care of the business matters," Elizabeth said and closed the door behind her, bidding Rosa farewell. Al made several heavy advances and overtures toward Rosa, but she remained cold and aloof. She made sure he would not get anywhere with her.

She was at home in time to talk to Jake at the scheduled time and agreed to meet once a month at Manuel's where she would give him three hundred dollars for the next ten months. They would also discuss their likes and dislikes, knowing the Immigration and Naturalization Service would question them in detail once she applied for her permanent residency and citizenship. It was important they knew about each other's family, where they met, and how long they had dated. Jake kept these meetings as brief as possible. He just wanted the money, and was vague when conveying issues regarding himself.

Eva replaced Carmen at the motel, and was looking for somewhere to live. She moved in with Rosa but it was a less than ideal relationship. Neither cared for the other. Both went their separate ways, but given the economic necessity, they needed each other. At least Eva enabled Rosa to remain in her cheap apartment.

Rosa held fast to her dream of becoming a citizen. One day she would be able to step out of the shadows and find work where she would be paid a decent wage and treated with respect. There were many places on the Las Vegas Strip and in the posh hotels where she could work. Maybe she could even work as a hostess in a fine dining establishment. Those dreams kept her going, with the hope that she would one day be able to bring her beloved *'esposo y ninos'* to America.

Occasionally Elizabeth slipped her an extra twenty dollars and gave her some old clothes. Rosa felt fortunate and grateful that the señora was so good to her. She also kept out of Al's way as much as possible as he always made a play for her.

Finally, it was the day before her wedding at the chapel. She didn't care that she would be marrying someone else while already married. Jake was a means to an end. She knew that as soon as she was a citizen, she would neither see nor hear from him again. She was startled by the phone ringing and hoped she was not being called to work on Saturday. It was Jake.

"Bring an extra five hundred dollars tomorrow," he said curtly.

"I can't get that kind of money," Rosa wailed. She was bewildered.

"Bring it or the deal's off," Jake said threateningly and hung up.

Rosa sat on the side of the bed and buried her face in her hands, crying uncontrollably. She thought of Elizabeth. Yes, Elizabeth would help her. She ran down to the bus stop hoping to catch the bus, and luckily, being Friday and rush hour, the buses were always late. To pass the time, Rosa looked at the assorted items in the pawn shop window. It seemed an eternity, but she was soon ringing the front door bell at the Baines house. It was dusk.

Al answered the door, drink in one hand, cigar in the other.

"Where's Señora Baines?" asked Rosa timidly.

"She's gone to her sister's for the weekend," he slurred, beckoning her inside. He had been drinking heavily. "What are you doing here?"

Rosa's hopes were dashed. All her planning was about to come crashing down. She knew it would be hard to get the money from Al.

"I need five hundred dollars," she blurted out boldly. Al's laugh was menacing. "I need it tonight and I will do anything," Rosa continued, undaunted. "I will work for you for the next six months for nothing. I beg you, Señor Baines. Please, just give me the money."

Al reveled in the irony of the situation. Rosa had always given him the cold shoulder and now she was begging him. Now she could make it up to him. He slowly lay back on the couch with his feet up.

"Well, there is something you can do for me," he sneered, as he removed his wallet tauntingly revealing some bills. "I think you know what it is."

She knew exactly. She bit her lip and tried to think fast. She knew it was her only hope of having the money for Jake the next day. She paused.

She lowered her eyes in shame and stiltedly started to unbutton her dress. It fell to the ground. There was total silence.

"Go on," Al said slowly, still puffing on his cigar, and putting his wallet on the coffee table. She slowly removed her slip and the rest of her garments and stood totally naked in front of him, feeling nothing but humiliation. He had degraded her. She tried to think of her husband and boys and how important her family was. This situation would soon pass. She would never come back to this house again. All these thoughts flashed through her mind.

She was snapped back to reality when Al said, "That's more like it. Why don't you run upstairs to the bedroom while I mix us some drinks?" He turned and stumbled toward the cocktail room next door, and she heard him emptying ice cubes into his glass. She only had a few minutes. Leaving her petticoat on the floor, she quickly threw on her dress. She looked in the wallet and snatched the cash—all three hundred dollars. Frantically, she grabbed a small crystal clock on the mantel, and ran as fast as she could toward the front door.

By now, it was dark outside, which was good. She ran for several blocks and stumbled upon a small park, where she sat breathless for a while. She needed to think. She still did not have the five hundred dollars. Again, she waited for what seemed like forever before the bus arrived. The bus stopped at the pawn shop five minutes before closing. She haggled with the broker, but he only offered her one hundred and fifty dollars for the clock. She pleaded for more, but he stubbornly gave her three fifty-dollar bills.

"I need another fifty dollars," she begged.

"I'll give you fifty dollars for the ring on your hand," he said flatly.

Time was running out. It was her wedding ring, the only

possession she had that her husband had given her. She sobbed as she handed over the ring. She cried on the bus all the way back to her apartment, and fell asleep crying. What had she done? Her dream would finally come true, but at what cost?

She entered the chapel to see Jake seated in the front row. "Where's the money?" he growled. She could not believe how cold he was. She pulled the five hundred dollars from her purse, which he snatched from her hand and then pushed her away. As she fell to the floor, he ran out of the chapel, stuffing the money into his denim pockets. One of the fifty-dollar bills fell to the ground as he stumbled down the steps heading toward the street.

Buster barked furiously and scampered out into the driveway, heading for the street as fast as his short, stubby legs could carry him. Rosemary ran into the chapel and picked Rosa up from the floor where she lay sobbing, almost hysterical. She was in a daze. She had no idea where Jake lived. She realized that all the information he gave her had probably been phony. Rosa let her story tumble out from her. Between the tears and crying, she described her job and her apartment, Al and Jake, how she stole and finally had to sell her wedding ring, and how her dream had now turned into a nightmare. Rosemary held Rosa in her arms and rocked her gently, trying to quiet her.

"There now," she said comfortingly, stroking Rosa's hair.

Buster wandered slowly back toward the chapel, sniffing the fifty-dollar bill as he reached the chapel steps. He picked it up with his teeth, and slowly made his way toward Rosemary and Rosa. He dropped the note at Rosa's feet and nudged her gently.

Rosa looked down, eyeing the bill. Rosemary leaned over

and picked it up, and wiping the tears from Rosa's face, said, "This will at least get your wedding ring back. It's a start." She smiled wanly.

Heartbroken, Rosa nodded forlornly, "*Si*. Is a start."

Chapter 8

Doubling Down

Lester and Chester were identical twins in every way but one. Their brains controlled the opposite sides of their bodies. Lester wrote with his left hand, and Chester wrote with his right. Lester always sat on the left side of the sofa while Chester gravitated to the right. But otherwise, they were identical. It had been that way since they were kids at school in Colorado. They dressed the same, indulged in the same hobbies and always, but always, ordered the same food at restaurants.

However, theirs was a relatively isolated world. Most other school children viewed them warily. They confused their schoolmates at sports and played constant pranks to fool the little girls. This separated them from their peers, but having each other, they were never lonely and were always able to count on each other. It was a dependency that took them from childhood through adolescence into their adult lives. Their teenage years created a little turbulence, as they were both always attracted to the same girl, causing the only continual source of disagreement between them. They resigned themselves to a life of co-existence, knowing that marriage would never be in the cards.

Both Lester and Chester were academically challenged at school. Neither really excelled at anything. But both were expert card players and decided to move to Las Vegas where they were hired as blackjack dealers at one of the major casinos. Management understood their need for proximity to each other, and accommodated them accordingly. They were always scheduled for the same shift and positioned at adjacent tables—Lester on the left and Chester on the right. They worked best when together and the management observed how deftly the cards were dealt when Lester and Chester were stationed alongside each other. There was a natural comfort level. Over a period of time, they were moved up to the high roller tables which, given their natural abilities and dexterity, were always full of customers.

Lester and Chester established a remarkable *modus vivendi*. They shared a modest apartment on a tree-lined street in a relatively isolated suburban part of Las Vegas. It was sparsely furnished with a well-worn sofa and loveseat in the living room that also housed a small wooden coffee table and a large screen TV. A few bland pictures hung unevenly on the walls revealing nothing about the individuals who occupied the apartment. There was one bedroom with twin beds and a bathroom with twin sinks, where they could keep their own toiletries—Lester's on the left and Chester's on the right. The apartment had a little functional kitchen with a small dining table that could accommodate four comfortably. The apartment served their purposes.

They arranged to alternate the cooking and driving. The week one drove to work, the other cooked the meals. Saturday morning they shopped for groceries together, then spent the afternoon cleaning the apartment. Saturday evening they enjoyed a night out on the town, which consisted of taking in a movie or dining out, either at a pizza parlor or the local

Chinese restaurant. Sunday was sports day. They watched sports from early morning to late at night. The TV remote controls were perched on both ends of the couch for them to switch channels whenever there was a more important game. Typically, Lester was a fraction ahead of Chester when it came to flicking the channels. They both knew to switch to the same game, though, and it never caused any problems. They were both sports addicts and watched basketball, baseball, football, ice hockey, whatever was showing, while swigging back their beers and munching on the chips and dip.

During commercial breaks they both tried and completed the soduku in the *Review-Journal*, which delivered two copies to their home daily. They enjoyed playing with numbers, and it helped keep their brains agile for their dealing. Their life was relatively routine, some would even say humdrum. But it was one in which they were both able to function and enjoy. Their lives may not have been exhilarating, but they were content.

One Saturday they both read in the newspaper about a line dance and square dance group that met in their neighborhood. The advertisement was repeated every week, and they had seen it before, but had never given dancing a thought. So, in a rare move of bold adventurism, they decided to do something different and try it out. The first night was free, so they had nothing to lose. If they didn't enjoy it, they could always leave and head off to the pizza parlor.

They ventured into the dance hall five minutes before the advertised commencement time and stood absolutely astonished, their jaws dropped. Sitting against the wall across the room Dolly and Molly smiled demurely at them in their identical red gingham skirts, frilly white blouses, and little red bows above bangs in their dark, cropped hair. The coy young ladies were identical.

Lester and Chester made a beeline over to where Dolly and Molly were sitting and introduced themselves. The girls blushed. Lester went straight for Dolly, who was seated on the left, and Chester parked himself in front of Molly, seated on the right. It was love at first sight for them all. Dolly and Molly were not ravishing beauties—in fact, they were relatively plain looking—but Lester and Chester identified with them immediately. There were unspoken bonds and understandings.

While still in their teens, Dolly and Molly had moved from Iowa to Las Vegas with their parents. They knew only too well what Lester and Chester had endured through school, having suffered the same fate—especially as it related to dating. Dolly and Molly almost always fell for the same guy. But most of the time, dating was pretty non-existent for them. Once a guy saw they were twins, he stayed away. It was too confusing and too complicated. Neither girl attended the high school prom or dated any boy more than once. This was as much their own doing, as neither twin liked to be apart from the other for any length of time.

Dolly and Molly, too, were average students, and had no desire to extend their education beyond high school. They both worked at the box office of one of the casino showrooms, which entitled them to free passes for all the concerts that played the showroom. Both were star struck and enjoyed the parade of singers, dancers, and comedians that passed through the venue where they worked.

"It's time to grab your partners and head to the dance floor," yelled the caller gaily from the stage, where the twang sound of country and western music started playing. The four headed to the center of the floor and faced the confused and amused looks of other dancers. They were used to being looked at, though, and now they had partners with whom they could relate. None could remember when they had so much fun.

They agreed to meet on Monday evening to go to a movie. Lester and Chester picked up Dolly and Molly from their home, headed toward the local Cineplex, and purchased tickets for the comedy showing. Lester and Chester carried the cardboard trays holding their hotdogs, candies, popcorn, and extra large sodas. But when they arrived at the aisle, confusion arose. Who would sit next to whom? Lester wanted to sit with Dolly on his left and Chester on his right. Chester wanted Lester on his left and Molly on his right. But it was unthinkable to Dolly and Molly to sit through a two-hour movie separated from each other. It had never happened in their lives. So it had been with Lester and Chester. No way could they sit apart for two whole hours. They always sat next to each other at sports events and movies. They struggled at the aisle trying to devise an acceptable seating arrangement.

"Hey you! Will you sit down and shut up?" came the muffled demand from someone a few rows back. They turned to see an already overweight man stuffing his face with a large hamburger.

"What's yer problem?" hollered another.

The four tiptoed back to the lobby of the movie complex to discuss a compromise. The beauty was they all understood the difficulty each of them was facing. Ultimately, they arrived at a relatively workable solution. Dolly and Molly would sit next to each other in the row and seats directly in front of where Lester and Chester would sit. It was less than ideal, but it worked for all of them. It became the game plan for all subsequent outings to movies, sports events, and concerts.

Restaurants were different. They always demanded a square table where Lester could sit next to Dolly and Chester, and Chester could also sit next to Lester and Molly. Dolly and Molly were then also positioned to sit next to each other.

The four became inseparable. Evenings when nothing was planned, they alternated dinner at each other's homes. Both dining room tables were square and they were able to use their assigned restaurant seating formula to everyone's satisfaction. After dinner they chatted and played pinochle or poker. Dolly and Molly were often able to obtain extra entertainment passes to the shows at the showroom where they worked, but unless they could locate tickets where they could sit directly in front of Lester and Chester, they passed on the opportunity.

They continued dancing, though they were all more comfortable participating in the line dancing than square dancing. During square dancing, they insisted on being in the same square, which confused and befuddled the others in the square. The other four dancers never knew who they were dancing with, and frequently the squares involving the twins broke down, much to the irritation of the other two couples.

It was just a matter of time before the question of marriage arose. It was a delicate subject that no one wanted to broach. Lester had finally found the girl of his dreams in Dolly. But going through life without Chester at his side would be like walking around with his right arm and leg missing. Chester dearly loved Molly, but felt the same way about Lester— except with his left arm and left leg missing. Dolly and Molly

The Chapel of Eternal Love

realized that Chester and Lester were their only real chance for happiness with a member of the opposite sex, but balked about having to spend their lives without each other. Neither would let that happen. They were too attached to each other.

Both couples found themselves head over heels in love. It was something that none of them had ever really dreamed of or contemplated. This could be their last chance for real true happiness and they all knew it. How long could they continue being together—yet apart? They moved into a duplex where Dolly and Molly had the one unit and Lester and Chester rented the other. But it was a short-term solution and only delayed the inevitable.

Finally they decided to rent a two-bedroom apartment into which they all moved, much to the extreme annoyance of Dolly and Molly's parents. They didn't understand anyway, rationalized Dolly and Molly. They had no concept of what it was like for the girls growing up as identical twins. Living together worked out superbly for all of them and none had ever been happier. Their lives were totally blissful except for one thing—the marriage commitment. The girls especially dreamed of being married.

The Chapel of Eternal Love was the perfect setting to right that wrong, and the four of them duly pulled into the driveway in Lester and Chester's car, laughing and reveling in their happiness. The men wore yellow polyester leisure suits, which was very formal for them, and the ladies, identical lemon gingham dresses. Dolly and Molly were both very fond of gingham.

Bemused, Rosemary smiled as she signed them in the registry and helped them with their paperwork. They all chattered and bickered gently with each other as to what to fill out on the forms. She thought the couples looked very cute—although she didn't know who was marrying whom—but her hunches told her they would all have a happy future together. She was able to calm the confusion, and complimented the ladies on their dresses, who thanked her coyly. Buster moved from one paw to the other, not knowing who was who or what was what. He started running round in circles as if chasing his tail. He was befuddled by the situation, but barked gaily, joining in the festivity of the pairs.

Hand-in-hand the couples, chatting excitedly, walked hastily under the archway and into the chapel, taking their places at the altar. Dolly and Molly in the front, with Lester and Chester standing next to each other slightly behind them—Lester on the left and Chester on the right.

Chapter 9
It's a Gamble

Buster lapped some water from his bowl, then flopped onto his blanket in the corner of the office. He was exhausted. It had been a full day already and it was nap time. His ears barely moved as the soft, gentle purr of the Rolls Royce pulled into the driveway.

Rosemary knew it had to be her old friend, Pru, whom she had not seen since high school. Naturally, she read about her in assorted newspaper articles over the years. But she was most surprised to receive a phone call from Pru's assistant booking the wedding appointment. Pru was probably unaware that Rosemary even worked at the chapel. She wondered if her friend would recognize her and if Pru was still as beautiful as she remembered.

She was. When the chauffeur opened the door to the Rolls Royce, Pru stepped out looking as serenely graceful and lovely as she always had been. Yes, age had taken its toll, but her kind, gentle face and soft blue eyes were still prevalent features. Her blond hair was now slightly silvery.

Exuding a quiet and calm exterior, Pru had cultivated nerves of tempered steel. Almost twenty years before, her husband had been killed in a plane crash, leaving her a wealthy widow at an extremely young age. She had inherited the vast hotel empire that her husband had forged and worked hard to create. Not having any prior business experience, Pru was forced to learn the business as rapidly as she could, and had managed to maintain the reputation of the hotels as one of elegance and excellence. Given her shy and retiring temperament, it was no small feat. She retained the services of most of her husband's top advisors, lawyers, accountants and management team, whom she rewarded handsomely, though their loyalty, respect and trust was demanded in return. Those who failed were cut loose with the speed of a laser beam. Fortunately, most of the people in her employ admired the business acumen she had developed. They also appreciated her kindness and sense of fairness. Advised of any real hardships that her employees were suffering in their private lives as well as any significant happy events she wrote fitting notes, accompanied by small appropriate gifts.

Rosemary stepped out from the office to welcome her old friend and was delighted at the embrace and remembrance that Pru displayed. Rosemary eyed the young man exiting from the passenger side of the car, struck by his good-looking features. *How nice that her son would be a witness to the wedding*, Rosemary thought, not remembering that Pru even had a son. The young man strode to Pru's side and passionately kissed her on the lips. The man alongside her friend was definitely not her son.

"You must meet my future husband, Chad," Pru enlightened her friend. After the brief introduction, Chad excused himself to the restroom. Pru must have read the expression of concern on Rosemary's face.

"I know. It's a gamble," she stated, as the two locked arms and walked toward the office. "But he does make me happy,

Rosemary. And I *do* love him," she continued.

"Well, as long as you love him and he loves you, I guess that's really all that matters," Rosemary responded ambivalently, deciding to keep her many questions and reservations to herself.

It had been a tough time for Pru since her husband died. True, the business was rewarding, but the nights were lonely, and the vast penthouse suite she occupied at her luxury Las Vegas hotel was empty. She had never entertained the idea of remarrying, or even having a lover. She knew she would never have another love like she'd already had with her husband. But then, she had never planned on meeting Chad.

Pru always enjoyed playing Chemin De Fer while staying at one of her casino-hotels in Monte Carlo, and enjoyed Baccarat, its American counterpart, when she was in Las Vegas. Often, when she was feeling particularly lonely, she would signal downstairs to the casino, leave her penthouse suite and head for the Baccarat room, where a seat was always reserved should she decide to participate at a moment's notice, which was often. Without asking, her favorite cocktail, a Cosmopolitan, was always brought to her spot at the table.

One evening, she was barely seated, when she looked across the table and observed a young man, the epitome of a Giorgio Armani model. Chad was impeccably dressed, with well-manicured hands and a suave, rugged masculinity. He had her favorite combination of dark hair and penetrating blue eyes. As he held her gaze, she was embarrassed by her heartbeat and tried in vain to ignore the man, who was clearly several years her junior. She endeavored to concentrate on her card game, but felt his focused eyes undressing her from afar. She casually glanced at him again and sensed how much he wanted her. She was surprisingly excited, flattered by his obvious attention. He flirted seductively, raising his glass to her whenever she won. She noticed how much he was losing at the table, and admired the nonchalant manner in which he seemed to handle his losses. To lose so graciously exuded class. She had never seen Chad at her hotel before, and her intuition and radar dictated she run a routine background check.

The next day, Pru was disappointed, and yet, somewhat not surprised with the report from her detective. Chad was very well known among many casinos as a very heavy gambler whose debts had been covered over the years by a variety of extremely wealthy widows. A knife struck in her heart. He was the sole person with whom she had an ounce of interest since the loss of her husband, and she discovered that he was nothing more than a common gigolo. A man who earned his living off the misery of women. She thanked her loyal detective for his fast work.

Still, she could not get Chad out of her mind. There was always the possibility that he might not return to the casino. She hoped this would be the case and that she would be able to dismiss him from her mind so easily.

However, curiosity got the better of Pru, so she returned to the table of the previous evening's encounter. She was relieved, in a sense, when she did not see him seated there, and started to play her cards and sip her Cosmopolitan. Her mind told her it was a good thing, yet in her heart, she was crestfallen. She opened her handbag and pulled a cigarette from the gold cigarette case, and was taken aback as a man's hand flicking a lighter appeared at the end of the cigarette. She allowed the cigarette to be lit, and, recognizing the beautifully manicured hands from the night before, turned her head to view the obvious gentleman, whose subtle cologne she now enjoyed. Chad's smile and those piercing blue eyes greeted her. She admired his perfect chiseled face and his taste in magnificently tailored suits. In all probability, his clothes had been selected by a wealthy widow, she realized. She nodded slightly and thanked him.

"Let me assure you, the pleasure was all mine," Chad responded in his best seductive manner. "May I also have the pleasure of buying you dinner?"

"Oh, I don't think so," Pru responded, somewhat embarrassed.

"Why not? You know you want to," Chad continued, knowing he was in command of the situation and that Pru would not be able to resist him. No woman ever had.

Pru was unaccustomed to such forthrightness. Her mind told her to decline the offer, but her heart instructed her to take the gamble. This time Pru followed her heart. She nodded and gathered her wrap, which Chad placed around her shoulders and escorted her to the five-star French restaurant in her hotel. She was determined he would pay the bill. He would not seduce her to the point where she would be next in the line of wealthy widows whom he had conquered, and presumably whose hearts he had broken. She kept what had been learned of his past to herself, while clearly, he knew exactly who she was. Attempting to remain distant, his very being fascinated her.

The evening was surprisingly enjoyable for her, and the conversation flowed smoothly. They both held a penchant for opera, ballet, and classical music, and they discussed many composers, opera singers, and ballet dancers. She was impressed with his in-depth knowledge. He was the perfect gentleman the entire evening. She was pleasantly taken aback when he hastily reached for the check as soon as it arrived and paid with cash. *Thank goodness it was not the credit card of one of his mistresses,* she thought. He seemed genuinely interested in her, but she was uncertain as to whether that was his style...his technique of luring women into his den. He escorted her to the elevator, where he kissed her hand tenderly, and bade her good night.

Pru tossed and turned in her bed that evening, hardly sleeping at all. She felt lonelier than ever, and hungered for the touch of this man who made her feel so desirable. She wished she knew how sincere his overtures were and how much was just a game to him. She was annoyed at herself and confused, having always been so calm and in control. But where had it taken her? A solitary life in an empty penthouse.

Pru was touched the next day when a huge bouquet of two dozen roses arrived at her office. The card read simply, "Thank you for the pleasure of your company. May I have the honor again soon? Chad." She had to see him again. He had her all tied in knots. Shortly after the flowers arrived, her assistant buzzed through to her office.

"There's a Chad on the line for you. He says the call is personal."

Pru took the call. Chad wanted to take her out for dinner again. But deciding to take control of the situation, Pru invited him to her penthouse suite for dinner. There she would be in command, could confront him with what she knew about his life, and see his reaction. She was not like one of his ex-lovers. She was a fairly shrewd judge of character and how he responded to the confrontation would be a measure of whether she would pursue a friendship, let alone anything beyond.

Chad arrived punctually, with a small gift box, elegantly wrapped, for her. Pru opened the gift to discover a small music box with a ballerina on top. When she wound the key to the music box, the ballerina twirled as the music played Chopin's "Nocturne." Deeply moved by his thoughtful and charming gesture, she fought back the tears welling up. But before his gift could be accepted, she had to know of his past—and needed to hear it from Chad.

Before she even had time to phrase the question, Chad took her by the hands and looked directly into her eyes, and said "Pru, I have some confessions to make." Sitting across from her, holding her hands and looking her directly in the eye, he explained to her how he had lived off many women in the past, and also of his fairly severe gambling problem. When he saw her at the casino, he knew who she was, and he had intended to play her like the other women in his life. But somehow she was different. He really liked her for who she was. All the previous women anxiously took him to their bed the first night, and yet she had said farewell at the elevator. He was genuinely attracted to Pru and begged her forgiveness.

"I am not proud of my past. In fact, I'm ashamed of my life and want to start afresh. Above all, I wish to pursue our friendship. Please tell me you'll give us a chance," he implored.

She nodded. She found his candor refreshing. He intrigued her. Though initially he came across as very self-assured, there was now a very strong element of vulnerability about him. Pru listened intently, thinking about what he was telling her and willing to take a gamble with him.

Chad was offered a trial position in her customer relations department. Given his abundant charm, he was charged with ensuring that the needs of all the high rollers staying at her hotel in Las Vegas were met. He was to keep them happy at all costs and she could certainly keep her eye on him. As a condition of his employment, Pru insisted he attend Gamblers Anonymous meetings. Her detective was also commissioned to routinely check on Chad. To her pleasant surprise, Chad attended his gamblers meetings regularly. He also, apparently, was being faithful to her. The private eye reported no romantic dates or dinners with any other females.

As the months passed, she was impressed with the finesse with which Chad handled the problems that came across his desk, and the glowing compliments from the high roller guests were reassuring. He was obviously an asset to the hotel and was having a positive impact.

Occasionally Pru asked Chad to accompany her on trips to her other hotels. Both especially relished the forays to New York and San Francisco, where they delighted in countless evenings attending the symphony concerts and operatic events at the New York Met. Their souls were in total harmony at any musical happening. It was more than a love for both of them. It was a passion. He often surprised her with tickets he had purchased for the Met. She knew they were not cheap and that they consumed a fair amount of his paycheck. Clearly, he was not using her. She allowed him to pay as often as possible, as she knew he was learning how much more pleasurable it was to give than to receive.

After six months of courtship, Chad finally proposed to her. He knew he could offer her nothing that she did not already have. But he was very protective of her and, above all, he was able to give her his undying and unconditional love and loyalty—and he *did* respect her. For his part, he knew he no longer needed to win at cards. He had won her heart.

Pru was willing to take the gamble. Neither wanted a large wedding. Pru was too shy and modest to be the center of attention. It would just be a quiet affair with the two of them.

Now, here they were at the Chapel of Eternal Love. Rosemary was a witness to their nuptials, and was genuinely pleased, if not a little apprehensive, for her old school friend. She felt the odds were for a successful marriage. But then, as Pru had rightly pointed out … "It's a gamble."

Chapter 10

The King Lives On!

Rosemary looked at her appointments. The next booking was unusual in more ways than one. Two couples renewing vows and one wedding had been registered in the log. She was curious as to the circumstances that would bring such a trio of couples to the chapel.

A Dodge minivan with a Tennessee license plate soon entered the parking area. Two smartly dressed couples in their mid fifties stepped down from the van, followed by a much younger couple, whom Rosemary assumed were the bride-and groom-to-be. The pretty young lady was dressed in long pale blue Hawaiian muumuu with a few plumeria flowers in her long flowing black hair that waved gently in the soft breeze. Rosemary noticed a Hawaiian lei draped round her neck, as well as around the necks of the other members of the wedding party. Suddenly, the presumed husband came into her full view. *He looked the image of Elvis*, she thought, with the inimitable hairstyle and dark sunglasses. His pale blue, open-necked leisure suit with its many rhinestones down the sides of the trouser legs matched in color with the bride's ensemble.

She figured this was one of her infrequent Elvis style weddings. There were a few Elvis-themed wedding chapels in Las Vegas, and she often wondered why those would not be chosen over hers for such marriages, but the couples who came to her chapel always seemed to have their reasons.

Today was a very special occasion. It was the silver wedding anniversary for both sets of parents, who had enjoyed a double wedding at the Chapel of Eternal Love twenty-five years ago to the day and wished to renew their wedding vows. Now their children were marrying and wanted to be married at the same venue. It was an awesome moment as they all stood outside the chapel—especially the parents. The chapel was just as they remembered it, as if it had been arrested in time. The memories the chapel invoked were incredible.

Mavis, Bobby, Val, and Mike had met years before they married. Each had managed the chapters of their local Elvis Presley fan clubs in various parts of the mid-west, writing and telephoning each other frequently. This was during an era before email and the internet made communication so much simpler. They met when they all travelled to Las Vegas to see Elvis' engagement in December 1976 at the Hilton Hotel. For Mavis and Val—who were the same age—the trip, hotel, and concert tickets were a twenty-first birthday present from their parents. Bobby and Mike had saved hard from their jobs in order to make the trip. The quartet was excited to have good tickets to the shows and to be sharing adjacent seats. Even though they knew members from other chapters of the fan club, these four established a close-knit bond.

Little did they realize as they watched that final concert on December 12, that it would be the last time The King would ever be seen in concert in Las Vegas again. Sure, they had seen him on his tour in 1977 and had previously experienced Elvis in concert at other venues, but all agreed, there was nothing like The King appearing in the heart of the Nevada desert.

There seemed to be so much more razzmatazz when he was in Vegas. Maybe it was just the energy that Las Vegas embodied.

Naturally, they were devastated when the tragic news exploded on August 16, 1977 of The King's premature death. He had been a major part of all of their lives for so long. They had grown up with his music and his movies. It was inconceivable there would be no more Elvis. They dutifully made the pilgrimage to Graceland and took part in the vigil, which they continued to do every year after his death. Elvis' passing took with him their innocent childhood memories and a large part of their lives in general.

But through their sorrow, the bond between Mavis, Bobby, Val, and Mike grew stronger. Over a period of time a developing love between Mavis and Bobby evolved, as it did with Val and Mike. They became couples, and the couples became the best of friends. After brief engagements, they decided on a double wedding in Las Vegas, where they could relive the memories of their last visit. By staying at the Hilton, maybe they could recapture the ecstasy of the special concerts they had been privileged to see and that had brought them so much joy and happiness; now just vivid memories. But somehow, it did not seem right at that time to marry at one of the Elvis-related wedding chapels, so they opted instead for the Chapel of Eternal Love. They discussed having an Elvis impersonator perform at the wedding, but it was too soon after The King's death. They figured it would be disrespectful. Their mourning period had yet to pass.

The two couples moved to Memphis, Tennessee, where they could be closer to each other, to their idol, and to Graceland. A year later, Mavis gave birth to a boy, who was naturally named Elvis, and a few months later, Val and Mike became the proud parents of a baby girl whom they christened Priscilla. Fortunately, Elvis and Cilla, as she would be called by friends and family, became fans of The King as they were growing up. Not that they had much choice.

Both sets of parents' houses were shrines with pictures, posters, clocks, mugs, and other Elvis memorabilia displayed prominently throughout their homes. Some of the items were rare and valuable collectors' items, while others were gimmicky and cheap souvenirs. With the advent of videos and subsequently DVDs, most Sundays were spent watching reruns of Elvis movies, TV appearances and concerts. They knew the words to all the movies by heart. Elvis and Cilla joined the time-consuming family hobby, answering the emails to the members of the fan club. Ironically, the membership of their fan club chapter grew with the passage of time, as opposed to diminishing, which did not surprise the devotees one iota.

As a joint celebration, when Val and Mavis both turned fifty, the families planned a trip to Germany where Elvis had spent time in the military. They hired a van travelling and touring round Friedberg, Bad Nauheim, Wiesbaden, and other haunts that Elvis might have visited during his army service. They made a point of including some of the locations where *G.I. Blues* was filmed, even though they were all aware Elvis had not filmed any part of the movie until he returned to America.

Elvis and Cilla originally planned on being married in Hawaii, the location of their favorite Elvis movie, *Blue Hawaii*. It was the one place they both dreamed of visiting, but the families talked them out of the plan. Far better they follow the footsteps of the parents and marry in Las Vegas, they reasoned. Cilla and Elvis could then honeymoon in Hawaii. The trip to Hawaii would be the wedding gift from both sets of parents.

They all arrived in Nevada the day before the wedding and checked into the Hilton Hotel, which to the parents, still brought back beautifully haunting memories of The King. They stood at the Elvis statue near the lobby of the hotel, and clicked their cameras incessantly with pose after pose of various combinations of the groups and couples present. What wonderful wedding souvenirs, they all thought. Cilla and Elvis were treated to the wax museum where more photos were taken alongside the lifelike waxwork of Elvis.

Mavis, Bobby, Val, and Mike were disappointed that Elvis and Cilla would not be able to visit the Elvisarama Museum just off the strip that had closed a few years earlier. It would have been a fitting venue for the day before the wedding and surely a highlight of their stay in Sin City.

Now they were all huddled in Rosemary's office. Buster awoke to the raucous sound of all the parties speaking at once. He sneezed and, confused by the commotion, decided to sit on his rug and observe the proceedings from a safe distance.

Where was the singer, they all wanted to know. Why was he late?

"Who did you ask to sing at your wedding?" Rosemary asked. Val fumbled in her purse, searching for the card. Rosemary was familiar with all the Elvis impersonators in the city.

"Don't worry he'll be here," Rosemary reassured, upon seeing the card 'Kid Galahad—your electrifying Elvis impersonator.' "Please, have a seat in the chapel." She knew Gavin, the entertainer known as Kid Galahad. He always made a grand entrance with flair and panache. They would not be disappointed.

The group excitedly entered the chapel and arranged themselves in the front pews. The parents reminisced wildly about their experiences a quarter of a century ago, with conflicting memories of the events, almost forgetting that this was to be a big day for Cilla as well.

As if on cue, there was a loud twang at the entrance to the chapel. They all turned to face the most lifelike Elvis they had ever seen. It was Elvis in his hey-day—youthful, physically fit, distinctive hairstyle, clad in a tight-fitting red and black costume abundantly decorated with rhinestones. The ladies squealed in delight. He stood in the doorway, head down, one hand raised in the air, the other over the twine on the guitar. The similarity was haunting and scary.

He knew he had their attention and burst into the opening lines of "Viva Las Vegas" while gyrating his way to the front and center of the chapel. His presence totally dominated the atmosphere of the otherwise tranquil and reverent chapel, his performance uncanny.

Back in the office, Rosemary closed the door. Buster was crooning furiously, as if trying to sing. She had decided Buster's singing attempts were somehow connected to the sound emanating from the guitar, for the sounds of the piano, when it was used, never seemed to faze him. There was a pattern of Buster singing whenever a guitar was involved— usually at one of the Elvis weddings.

She tried in vain to quiet Buster so he would not be heard in the chapel and mar the event in progress. Fortunately, Gavin's opening number was always "Viva Las Vegas," which tended to drown Buster's out-of-tune attempts at harmonizing. Being totally familiar with Gavin's shtick, Rosemary prayed that the following two numbers, always selected by the bride and groom, would not be quiet ballads. She also hoped the bride and groom had not requested more than the standard fare.

Sadly, her prayers were unanswered, as she heard Gavin sing "Love Me Tender." It could have been a recording, he sounded so like Elvis. She placed Buster on her lap and stroked him. Still he howled. At the end of the song, she sat him on the floor, knowing the ceremony would take place before Gavin launched into his next number. The group had to be impressed. She knew they would be thrilled at their choice. How right she was.

Back in the chapel, they were enthralled.

"Awesome," Bobby kept repeating, and Michael nodded in agreement, grateful that they had hit the jackpot with Kid Galahad. Surely he had to be the best in town, they agreed. Cilla and Elvis were totally overcome by the emotion of it all, while Val and Mavis wiped tears from their eyes marveling at all the memories that were evoked. They were overwhelmed.

At the request of Cilla and Elvis, Kid Galahad started to sing romantically, "This is the moment I've waited for. I can hear my heart sing ..." It was the "Hawaiian Wedding Song," Cilla and Elvis' all-time favorite. Kid Galahad stood in front of the altar with Elvis and Cilla clasping their hands together in front of him. They gazed lovingly into each other's eyes and savored their special moment, knowing they would be visiting the tropical paradise the next day.

Instead of the customary ceremony, Elvis and Cilla had elected to recite their wedding vows to the lyrics of the favorite Elvis song of their parents, "The Wonder Of You", alternating the lines.

As Kid Galahad slowly slapped his thighs and softly strummed the tune, "When no one else can understand me," started Cilla.

"When everything I do is wrong," responded Elvis.

"You give me hope and consolation," Cilla chirped back lovingly.

"You give me strength to carry on," Elvis said, not missing a beat.

They both joined in reciting the remaining lines: "And you're always there, to lend a hand, in everything I do. That's the wonder, the wonder of you."

The parents stood at the pews and faced each other to hold hands. It was their time to be a part of the service and renew their vows, as they had promised and agreed. Kid Galahad upped the volume and the tempo a little for dramatic effect.

"And when you smile the world is brighter," the trio of ladies continued, going for the moment.

"You touch my hand and I'm a king," echoed the men.

"Your kiss to me is worth a fortune," fired back the ladies.

"Your love for me is everything," crooned the guys, passionately and sincerely.

All six joined together for the final verse, which ended in kissing and hugging.

As was the custom of The King, and knowing how to captivate an audience, Kid Galahad repeated the last chorus with a flourish for the grand finale.

Cilla and Elvis had a silver wedding gift for both sets of parents. They could no longer keep the secret and their excitement to themselves. When the kisses and hugs died down, Elvis proudly proclaimed, "We have some wonderful news for you on your special anniversaries."

"I'm expecting twin girls!" Cilla enthused euphorically. There were more hugs and kisses all round, as Elvis excitedly informed the delighted parents that the girls would be named Lisa and Marie after The King's daughter. The mothers wept.

As a bonus, Gavin sang "Crying In The Chapel" to the three joyous couples. After years of being an entertainer, he was prepared for any eventuality and surprise announcements.

As he opened with the all too familiar lines, "You saw me crying in the chapel. The tears I shed were tears of joy," Buster started to howl again in the office. Rosemary was unable to muzzle him.

The King lives on.

Chapter 11

Love Will Find a Way

Cory and Heidi had known each other for just over five years before arriving in Las Vegas for their wedding ceremony. They met while they were both students at Brigham Young University in Utah. Cory was in his final year and striving for his teaching degree. Heidi, one year younger and a year behind, was majoring in the Arts. Both lived away from home in separate small studio apartments off campus.

Cory was a shy, clean-cut youth and a practicing member of the Church of Latter Day Saints. He was born and raised in the small Utah town of St. George. It was initially at church where he had met Heidi, who had also been raised in the Mormon faith, a sweet, soft spoken, pretty girl who fell in love with Cory at first sight. She was resourceful and managed to cope, even if she was rather young to be living alone far away from her native Pennsylvania. Not that there was much for her there. Her mother and stepfather had always been active members of the Peace Corps, and were currently on assignment in Ghana. She formed an immediate bond with Cory and knew instantly she wished to share her life with him. Cory felt the same.

But both were pragmatic. Cory had already enlisted for a mission assignment in Bolivia for two years as soon as he graduated. The timing would allow for Heidi to complete her degree and work for a year, at which time her parents would be returning from Ghana. This would enable them to attend the wedding ceremony, which the couple had planned on being performed in the temple.

Cory and Heidi remembered distinctly the evening when they said their farewells. Heidi had driven him to the airport for his flight to Dallas-Fort Worth and then to South America. Pouring with rain, the windshield wipers flashed back and forth at a rapid pace. Cory was full of mixed emotions. His feelings of excitement and apprehension about his new venture in a far-off land and wishing Heidi would be alongside churned inside him. Heidi was very depressed, but managed a brave face. She knew Cory was fulfilling his duty. With her parents abroad, and now her boyfriend leaving, she felt very much alone.

A year earlier, before she'd even met Cory, Heidi had stopped at a convenience store late one night. Hidden from view by the displays in the corner of the store, she was unseen by the two new arrivals. Suddenly, there was an enormous commotion at the front counter. She heard the crash of glass as gunshots decimated the TV screen that would have recorded the presence of the interlopers. The store was being robbed. Heidi ducked to the floor, terrified for her life. Timidly peering up, she saw the robbers at an angle through the mirror on the ceiling in the far-off corner. Pointing her cell phone with its built-in camera toward the mirror, she clicked incessantly, hoping to record the faces of the robbers. She could see the terror in the face of the store clerk standing near the till with his hands up. Having grabbed the money, the robbers shot the attendant, who crumbled in a heap to the floor. A siren was heard in the distance and the robbers escaped in haste. Heidi sat on the floor screaming and sobbing uncontrollably as she relived the horror of the scene she had just witnessed. It had all happened so fast. She was dazed as they escorted her to the station where, as the sole witness to the crime, her statement and evidence was taken. It was a traumatic ordeal and she suffered nightmares for weeks after. She would now have to relive it for the jury.

Heidi decided not to tell Cory, as he would only worry, and not knowing how long the trial would last, she also knew Cory would insist on cancelling his mission. He couldn't do that. They had a plan. After a tearful farewell, Cory headed off to Bolivia, somewhere outside of La Paz.

The village where he was stationed was miles from anywhere and conditions were very primitive. Cell phones and computers were non-existent, and the village folk had never heard of the internet. There was not even a public telephone. Cory was to try and deliver his message to the rural communities and outer lying areas. His work was certainly a challenge. Although his Spanish was strong, the dialect spoken in this village was unfamiliar and communication was difficult. Still, he was determined to succeed. He wrote Heidi as regularly as the strict guidelines permitted, detailing his many different experiences. The program discouraged frequent correspondence, to focus on the higher purpose of the venture. Absence sure made his heart grow fonder, if that was possible, and he missed Heidi deeply.

Two years was going to be a long time. He was discouraged when no response was forthcoming and could not imagine why he had heard nothing as he eagerly awaited the infrequent mailbag deliveries. They were both so very much in love. The days and weeks turned into months, and still nothing. After a while, he stopped writing. As time passed, his hopes of marrying her dimmed, although his love for her never diminished or wavered.

After Cory's flight departed into the night, Heidi's life took a different turn. Drying her eyes, she slowly walked to her car and noticed a piece of paper on the windshield. She almost discarded it, thinking it was one of the advertisement flyers that are frequently cluttered under the wiper. But something made her read it. "DO NOT TESTIFY" the note stated, in differing sizes of print clipped from a newspaper. She quickly looked around to see if anyone was in sight. The parking lot was unusually silent, rain pounding on the concrete roof the only sound. Hurriedly, she climbed in the car and sped off as quickly as possible, heading for the police station where she was taken the night of the murder and robbery. She wished she had told Cory; she needed him now more than ever. The police were sympathetic but subjected her to a myriad of forms to complete. It was late when she returned home and tired as she was, she was unable to sleep.

Her fatigue made studies the next day at school almost impossible, and she departed for home a little earlier than usual. The light flashing on her answering machine excited her. She had hoped that it was the sound of Cory's voice telling her he had arrived safely. She panicked when she heard a muffled voice threatening her not to go to the police again.

Clearly, she was now being stalked. She kept herself locked in her apartment until daylight, again having a very sleepless night.

In the morning she felt nauseous and jumpy and went to her doctor for a prescription. Her doctor joyously gave her the surprising news that she was expecting a baby and sent her for an immediate checkup to the gynecologist in the next office. Heidi's head was spinning at this twist of events. She was euphoric at carrying Cory's baby but did not know how it would affect their future plans. How would he react?

She hoped her part in the trial would be over soon, so she could have a calm and stress free pregnancy. But what of the threats? She drove to the pharmacy for the prescribed pills, then home to reflect. She unlocked the door, and an eerie feeling overcame her. Nothing was out of place, but she cautiously and suspiciously moved through the rooms, finally arriving at the bathroom. She screamed when she saw the writing on the mirror in bright red lipstick. "Your baby will die, too!"

Fear gripping her, she ran from the house and drove straight to the police station. She could not go through with this. She was sick with worry. After what seemed an eternity, the station detectives and other officials came to the room, where she sat alone. She did not know who they were. After being escorted home to collect some items, she was taken, via an extremely devious route, to a hotel near the courthouse, where she was instructed to stay for the next few days and was provided with twenty-four hour surveillance. She was more concerned about the long term. She was determined to have Cory's baby. Oh, how she yearned for his presence and for him to hold her in his strong, reassuring arms and take away her anxiety. How could she manage it all alone?

The next day, Heidi received the devastating news that she was being placed in the federal witness protection program.

"No!" she shrieked in disbelief. "I can't, I can't! What about Cory? What about our baby?" she wailed plaintively.

"It's the only way, my dear." The female officer spoke softly, gently hugging her.

After the initial shock, Heidi surrendered to the protective and nurturing side of her nature. She now had someone else to think about. The welfare of her baby was of paramount importance and had to be the first priority in all her decision making. She knew she would be a good mother, and had planned on having a large family. The agency acted surprisingly swift. The day her testimony in the trial was completed, she was whisked to her apartment to gather a few necessary items of clothing, given a new identity, and escorted to the airport. She was unsure where she was going, but the agent had all the travelling documents and accompanied her to her final destination. She was somewhat concerned when she boarded a plane for Chicago, hoping she wasn't spending the rest of her life there. She was even more concerned when they subsequently travelled to La Guardia airport in New York. She did not care for huge metropolitan cities. Salt Lake City was as large as she cared for. Next she found herself headed to San Francisco where she boarded yet another flight to Juneau, Alaska, with the final flight delivering her to the quaint little town of Ketchikan. Heidi was exhausted, but was relieved when she arrived at the warm, inviting, cozy log home of Marion, where she would be staying.

Marion was in her mid fifties and was also a part of the witness protection program. "Welcome, Samantha," she said, extending her arms in a warm embrace. Heidi was taken aback. It was the first time anyone had called her by her new name. Marion was a strong, kind and reassuring woman. She owned a little souvenir store, "Port of Call" at the end of the main street, where Samantha was able to work before and after the baby was born.

When little Courtney was born, Samantha idolized her, and Marion assumed a natural grandmotherly role. As Marion was also separated from her loved one, the two women formed a deep and meaningful friendship and helped heal each other's heartaches. Samantha settled into her new life in Alaska and started rebuilding. She loved the town and community, but never lost her love for Cory. Her daughter was a permanent, daily reminder. There was so much of Cory in her little face already.

In the other hemisphere, Cory completed his mission in Bolivia. He returned to Salt Lake City in the hopes of finding Heidi, but all his resourceful efforts drew nothing but a blank. The University revealed none of the details of Heidi's parents. He did not even know her parents' surname. He only knew that she had a stepfather. Her disappearance was a mystery to their few friends. The ghost of Heidi haunted him wherever he went. He decided to follow in the footsteps of his would-be parents-in-law, and joined the Peace Corps for a two-year mission, assigned to teach school in Chile.

Taylor pushed his way through the security line at the Salt Lake City airport, frantic that he might miss his plane to Las Vegas.

"Excuse me, would you mind if I jumped in line ahead of you? I fear I might miss my flight," he implored of Cory who was forlornly reminiscing about the last time he departed from Salt Lake.

Cory beckoned the man to pass.

"Cheer up, young man!" The traveller observed Cory's wistful faraway look. "Where are you headed?"

"To Chile for a mission," Cory responded indifferently.

"Hmm! I think you should be going to Alaska, you know," he said matter-of-factly.

"Alaska?" said Cory inquisitively. "Why Alaska?"

"Ssh! I'm clairvoyant!" whispered Taylor, moving his luggage ahead. "I think you will find what you are looking for there. Mind you, Chile has its purpose, too," he continued. "At least you are headed somewhere exciting. I'm heading home to Las Vegas. Just been here visiting my cousin. Thanks for being so accommodating." He hastily placed his cases on the conveyor belt. "Be sure you heed what I say. Good things happen to good people." Then he disappeared through the security check and raced to the satellite building to board his plane.

Cory caught his flight and arrived in Valparaiso, Chile. He was greeted by the only other school teacher, and they caught the train to the small town in the northern part of Patagonia. Cory fell in love with the area and its pristine, natural beauty, and the little children at the school, so eager to learn. The place and people captured his soul, but his heart still yearned for Heidi. He spoke fluent Spanish, and the kids were devoted to him. Teaching was definitely his calling. If only he had his own children, though, he pondered forlornly. He wondered whether Heidi had discovered someone else, whether she was happy, whether she had a family.

Two years soon passed and he returned to Salt Lake City wondering where to take his life. Salt Lake had changed, he thought, but in reality it hadn't. He had changed. He had moved into a different culture that had captivated him, and he contemplated moving back there permanently. There was nothing for him in Utah.

It was a bold decision, and he needed to think on it. He had never forgotten the man's admonitions which, for some unknown reason, haunted him frequently. Maybe, he should visit Alaska first, he thought. He recalled the airport stranger's observation that "Chile would have its purpose." He sure had been right about that. A short vacation wouldn't hurt, Cory thought, and booked a week's cruise from Vancouver to mull his future.

Cruising was not for Cory, though. He was young, single, and a little shy. He felt alone as he wandered round the various ports of call. As the cruise ship turned at Juneau for the return journey, he wandered through the little town of Ketchikan, and thought it cute and charming. He was so immersed with the sights he failed to notice the time and heard the horn of the ship announcing the imminence of its departure. He rushed down the main street of the town, stopping in the little "Port of Call" souvenir shop for some postcards as mementos.

"That will be four dollars and thirty cents," said Marion, packing them in a little paper bag sporting an artistic logo with the store's name. Thanking her, he turned to leave.

"Sorry I'm late, Marion," Samantha said breathlessly as she dashed into the store, nearly knocking Cory over. They both gasped, staring at each other.

"Cory, is it really you?"

"Heidi!" Cory yelled joyously, as he grabbed her and spun her round in the air wildly.

When she heard Cory and Samantha talking excitedly over each other between the kisses, Marion ushered them hastily to the back storeroom. Courtney … baby … mission … Patagonia … murders … trials … she heard going back and forth. The ship's horn sounded its final warning. Cory rushed to collect his possessions from the ship to return to Heidi. He dashed downstairs to his cabin on the bottom deck, threw everything into his suitcase, and ran back to the gangway. Alas, it had already been raised. He reached in his case for the "Ports of Call" bag that held his postcards and saw the telephone number listed on the bottom. He had finally found Heidi. He had to get back to her. He couldn't lose her again. And he couldn't believe he had a child. He called Heidi from the ship, promising to speak to her when he arrived at Vancouver, which would be the next time the ship docked.

Cory needed to return to Salt Lake City. There was business to complete. He and Heidi could start a whole new life in Chile. They would be safe there. He would take care of everything. In a few short weeks, all arrangements were made.

They could no longer be married in the temple, and it was too risky for Heidi to return to Utah. The nearest big city was Las Vegas. Cory rented a car, drove down to the city that never sleeps, meeting Heidi and Courtney at McCarran International airport. He was overcome seeing his little girl for the first time; tears of joy rolled down his cheeks. How pretty she was, and so like her mother. Courtney ran to her father and hugged him. He held her tight in his arms. Heidi, too, cried tears of happiness and relief, as she now had both of her loves in her life. They sped off to the Chapel of Eternal Love, knowing they would soon need to be back at the airport for their flight to South America.

Buster observed them arriving from the top of the office steps and scampered behind the desk. He was not accustomed to children. The few he'd encountered tended to pull his ears and tail, causing him pain.

Cory and Heidi headed for the office, with little Courtney in the middle holding both her mother and her father's hands. Courtney was delighted to have a papa. The family could not have been happier.

Love had found a way.

Chapter 12

Looking Into the Future

What happens to a 'lady of the night' when the glamour fades and the years start taking their toll? That's what Sherri was asking herself as she looked in the mirror, removing her makeup. *What's to become of me?* She was panic-stricken.

She should have removed herself from the business years ago but had no other marketable skills, never having graduated from high school. The street was all she had ever known. Besides, the street had provided her with a reasonable income. She managed to be 'gainfully employed' for the best part of a quarter of a century, enough to pay her bills and keep her head above water. Never having been classy or beautiful enough to work the more glamorous casinos on the strip, for most of that time she had worked the same stretch of the street in Las Vegas, which was considered prime territory for the seedier part of the city.

She knew her days were numbered, however, when Charlie, her pimp, or 'caretaker' as Sherri liked to refer to him, moved her to a less desirable location. "You're just not doing the numbers, Babe," he had told her. "I need my best there," he said in his usual menacing tone.

He knew how to squeeze her out. She was not making the money in her prime location and certainly would not make it now in her new appointed spot. He wanted to see her squirm.

She was six months at her designated street corner, working longer hours for less money. She was barely making ends meet.

"You're not doing the numbers," Charlie constantly sneered at her.

"It's the location, Charlie," she'd retort. "Please give me my old territory back."

Finally, he decided to cut her loose. It was his experience that women in this business reached a certain age, and were more trouble than they were worth.

"But Charlie, I beg you, I'll do anything," she cried. "Tell you what. I'll give you 70-30 split. I promise," she pleaded.

"No dice, Babe. You're washed up. You're a has-been," he snarled, his voice oozing with contempt. The words struck like a dagger.

Sherri didn't understand why he was so hostile toward her. So she'd had her skirmishes. True, she'd been knocked around some, and he'd had to take her to the hospital on occasion and taken care of the bills. Yes, he'd had to bail her out of the clink from time to time. But no more frequently than any of his other girls. He had made heaps of money from her. He was supposed to be her 'caretaker.' That meant taking care of her. Now he was throwing her out? She couldn't comprehend. Having lived from hand to mouth instead of month to month, she struggled to find a job, depleting what little savings she had. She was almost down to her last dollar, when she was hired as a waitress in a small diner. It was not in the best part of town. But it was work, and only a bus ride away from where she lived. She eeked out enough from her pay and tips to keep going. Now, she was fired from that job, too.

As she stared at the mirror, with barely enough to pay her rent, her future looked very bleak indeed. She cried a little, feeling sorry for herself, before picking up the phone and calling the suicide hotline. She was not suicidal, but she needed to talk to someone. She had no friends and felt very alone.

"This is Taylor. How can I help this evening?" offered the warm, friendly voice at the other end of the line.

Taylor was a bachelor in his early fifties and a 'do-gooder.' Even he considered himself to be a bit of an eccentric, as did his workmates, who thought him more than a little odd. Taylor was not the most ambitious person imaginable. He coasted through life, living from day to day. He loved animals and spent four days a week working at the animal shelter, which paid a pittance, compensating his meager pay by doing clairvoyant readings two other days. He had to admit, though, that much of his claimed psychic ability was more gut feeling and guess work. He tried to read the cards, but his lack of repeat customers was indicative of his spotty ability. Truth to tell, he was probably a bit of a fraud. But he was a good natured, harmless soul who helped at the suicide prevention center one night a week, read to the elderly in a retirement home another night, and spent another evening at the local hospital with patients who received no visitors. The ashtray in his car was filled with dollar bills, which he handed out to the homeless on street corners when they ventured near him while waiting for the traffic lights to switch to green. In his free time, he loved to watch old black and white movies on TV, the golden age of Hollywood. In his view, nothing would ever come close to that classical era. He worked well with his colleagues but did not interact with them socially. He was very much a loner, and was happy that way. His life was fulfilling enough.

"I'm not suicidal," Sherri preempted. "I just need to talk to someone, that's all. I understand if you are too busy."

"That's why we're here," Taylor reassured. "What prompted you to call this evening?"

"I'm just feeling down and sorry for myself, I suppose. I lost my job today. I don't know if I'll get another. I don't even know how I can pay my rent." Sherri started to unload.

"What happened to your job?" Taylor inquired. "Maybe we can help find you another one?" he encouraged.

"I did something stupid," Sherri opined." I worked in a restaurant. It's in a crummy part of town, and a homeless woman came in. It was too awful. She had nothing and begged for something to eat. I gave her a bag with a couple of our pastries and a small jar of orange juice. Naturally, she couldn't pay so I gave it to her. The manager saw me and said it was tantamount to stealing, and fired me on the spot. That lady could be me in a few weeks time."

Taylor warmed to this woman's heart. Her compassionate spirit struck a chord with him. "Hmmm! I think I know just the one who can help. Ben, a colleague of mine here, owns a coffee shop. Not exactly up-market, but he might have something. Let me give him a call. Why don't you call me back in ten minutes?"

Sherri's hopes rose, as she hung up from this kind stranger. The minutes on her little bedside clock ticked slowly. As soon as the ten minutes were up, she dialed the number with mixed feelings of anxiety and trepidation, and was relieved when

Taylor answered the phone again.

"It's all set up. You have an interview with Ben at five tomorrow afternoon," he told her cheerfully.

"You're an angel of mercy," Sherri said thankfully.

"You'll do fine. I'm getting good vibes!" Taylor assured. He gave her directions and wished her good luck before hanging up.

Sherri was grateful the restaurant looked slightly better and busier than the one where she had previously worked. Ben was a short, slightly rotund individual with an affable manner. He greeted her in his office and invited her to talk about herself. Her experience in food establishments was somewhat minimal. Since he, too, worked at the suicide center, she hoped he would have a compassionate soul like Taylor's. She decided to be frank with Ben and 'fessed up about her past, how she came to work in a diner so late in life, and why she was let go.

She paused nervously to see how Ben would respond. The phone on his desk rang. After a brief silence, he said into the receiver, "What do you mean you can't make it in? Couldn't you have called me earlier? You know we are coming up to our busiest time of day." He hung up, clearly irritated by the conversation.

"Annie," he yelled. "Can you come here a minute?" Annie appeared at the door. "Can you cover for Patsy's shift? She's not coming in."

"Sorry, it's my turn with the kids this week. I have to go pick them up," Annie replied apologetically.

Ben turned to Sherri. "Would you like to start now?" he asked earnestly.

"Now?" she said in disbelief. "I'm not dressed for it. I …
I …"

"Annie will show you where the uniforms are and get you
a hairnet," Ben interrupted. "You'll work weekdays from four
to eleven. It's minimum pay, plus tips. We don't pool the tips
here. It's each to his own. Treat the customers well, they'll tip
you good. Treat them bad and you'll strike out. We have a
small profit-sharing plan, and minimal medical, but it's better
than nothing."

It's more than I ever had, Sherri thought.

Ben continued, "By the way, if you get any homeless
customers, send them round the back. All of our food is fresh,
and we give our day-old pastries to the homeless. Okay? Oh,
and wear a little less makeup, will you? What you were is not
what you are," he joked, trying to lighten the chat and make
Sherri feel at ease. "*And*," he emphasized, "I hope you can
handle a few rough customers."

As she followed Annie, she thought about what he
had said. In the restroom, she pursed her lips on a tissue to
remove some of the lipstick. *Handle rough customers indeed*, she
thought. She knew all about rough customers. She worked
hard the first evening, and Ben drove her home, thanking her
for stepping in and saving the day. She counted her tips and
was flabbergasted at how much she had made.

She waited a week, remembering the night Taylor worked
at the suicide center, and called him when she got home from
work.

"This is Taylor. How can I help this evening?" was the
now familiar sound.

"This is Sherri," she said, asking whether he remembered her.

"Of course I remember you. How did the interview go with Ben?"

She filled him in on how her week had been, and how much money she had made in tips. "I don't know how I can ever thank you. How I can repay you? You're a life saver."

"That's why we're here. I'm glad things worked out well. I figured you'd like Ben. He's a swell guy."

"Can I at least make you dinner?" Sherri asked, immediately wondering whether it sounded bold, and how Taylor would perceive her invite.

Taylor was moved. No one, but no one had ever offered to cook him a dinner since he left home. He thought for a moment, but knew the center discouraged fraternization.

"I'm quite a good cook, you know," Sherri tempted. "How about Saturday at six o'clock? I'll cook your favorite," she teased seductively.

Taylor decided to cast caution to the wind. "I have my last psychic reading at six. Can we do seven? And I love pot roast."

Sherri was surprised. "Pot roast it is. I didn't know you did psychic readings. What do you see for me in the future?"

"Can't say for sure right now. I'm really not that good," Taylor begged off, a little sheepishly.

Her doorbell rang at seven sharp. She glanced quickly around to ensure that everything was in its place. Her apartment was warm and inviting. Nothing fancy, but comfortable. The table was set simply with a small vase of flowers, and a candle flickering gently. A Frank Sinatra CD played softly in the background. She straightened her dress, and opened the door.

Taylor was no matinee idol in the looks department, she thought, but he was not a bad-looking dog. (And she knew about dogs, having encountered many over the years.) He was clean and presentable though, with a warm and genuine smile.

He handed her a relatively inexpensive bottle of red wine, then offered his hand forward for a handshake. He looked at her, and though her prettiness had been hardened presumably due to a very rough life, the lines gave her well-lived face a touch of character, he thought somewhat charitably. He could see her past just from her face, and from what Ben had told him.

He offered to pour the wine while she slipped into the kitchen to check on the food. The aroma of the pot roast indicated that she sure was a great cook. He surveyed the cozy and comfortable place, and the warmth that pervaded the atmosphere, especially enjoying her taste in music. He was quite a fan of the Rat Pack himself. Sherri returned to the small and compact living room, where they clinked their glasses in a toast. They discussed a myriad of subjects, laughing and joking and enjoying poignant serious moments as the evening passed. He loved the pot roast and vegetables she had cooked, as well as the home-baked apple pie and ice cream. It was good comfort food.

Sherri shared some of her life experiences with various anecdotes of her times at police stations and hospitals, which she explained with her usual self-deprecating humor. Taylor was non-judgmental. He knew that he was no prize, having his own idiosyncrasies. Sherri liked him, though. She felt relaxed and at ease, able to express her thanks for his being there for her at a time when she needed someone. Anyone.

Taylor could not remember when he had last enjoyed an evening so much. It was a refreshing change for him to be pampered and spoiled. He appreciated how attentively Sherri listened as he talked about his two pet dogs and his favorite black and white movies. He was familiar with some of the people Sherri had met at the hospital, since he knew the same nurses through his visitations. Sherri acted genuinely interested in him and his life.

The sound of Sinatra could still be heard; "I've got you under my skin" emanated from the speakers. "Come on, let's dance." Taylor pulled Sherri from her seat.

"I haven't danced in years," she said as he started to twirl her on the floor.

"Me either," he chuckled. "It's probably obvious!"

They both laughed as they sang along with Frank until the song finished. They both recognized the all-too familiar opening line to the next tune. "When somebody loves you ..." Sinatra crooned. They moved closer to each other and started to dance slower and the mood took on a more serious tone. "I *am* happy to be near you, Sherri," Taylor imparted, lifting her face to look at his. Sherri didn't respond. She didn't know what to say. She finally broke away and returned to the sofa.

"I just wanted to thank you, Taylor. You're a kind man. You're too good for me. This cannot go anywhere. You can never forget my past."

Taylor sat next to her and kissed her gently on her forehead. "I'm not concerned with your past. I'm looking into our future. Why don't you leave that to me?"

Sherri nodded, remaining silent.

Taylor rose to leave. "I had a wonderful, wonderful evening. Thank you."

She followed him to the door, where they exchanged a brief midnight kiss. Sherri watched his old dilapidated Ford car turn the corner at the end of the street and disappear, thinking she had made a friend.

They started sharing their weekends together and alternating dinners at each other's places. The first time she visited Taylor's modest and cluttered apartment, the dogs gave her a warm welcome. They were not used to company. She liked his pets, which was important to Taylor. Sometimes she helped with the cooking and cleaning up. Their evenings took on the tenor of comfortable friends more than passionate dates, but they had their romantic moments.

Despite having been surrounded by people all their lives, they had both always been alone. Now they had each other, and they enjoyed the same pleasures. Sometimes they spent a quiet afternoon just reading or watching one of Taylor's favorite black and white movies on TV. Occasionally, they took a drive to the strip or the mall or to some of the free exhibits in the various casinos.

The weeks turned into months and they soon celebrated their first anniversary together.

Taylor and Sherri were old souls. They were also two lost souls who had found each other, always looking forward to their next rendezvous every time they parted. Sherri treated and respected Taylor, like no other woman had. But Taylor felt he had nothing to offer Sherri. He had no savings and no job security. Having worked as long as Sherri had, he had equally as little to show for it. Nonetheless, he proposed to her, just offering himself. That was all Sherri wanted and needed.

He picked her up on the morning of their wedding and drove to the Chapel of Eternal Love. Sherri never dreamed of being a bride and was radiantly happy. Taylor thought she made a beautiful bride, and helped her out of the car and into the office. He looked pretty spiffy in his suit, Sherri observed, picking a speck of dust from his jacket.

Buster sniffed around Taylor's legs and wagged his tail. He recognized an animal lover. He dashed to his little food bowl and pulled a couple of doggie biscuits, which he dropped at Taylor's feet as if to express his gratitude.

"What a beautiful couple you are," complimented Rosemary, looking at the beaming couple.

"I don't know about that," joked Taylor bashfully.

"Ah, but beauty comes from within," she responded, knowing that this couple were all heart. She reached out and hugged them both.

As they walked toward the chapel, Cory and Heidi came out beaming with joy and pride, Cory holding little Courtney in his arms.

"Daddy, why is that lady wearing so much makeup?"

"Hush, Honey. That's not polite." Suddenly he recognized Taylor. He shook Taylor's hand firmly, and reminded Taylor of their encounter in Salt Lake City.

"You have changed my life. How did you know? How do you do it? How do you look into the future?"

Taylor shrugged as he struggled to recall their meeting. He was too happy to comment.

Heidi looked quizzically at her husband. "I'll explain later, Honey. Well, I hope your future will be as happy as I know ours will be," Cory declared. They headed toward his rental car to return to the airport.

"It will," smiled Taylor, as he put his arms lovingly and protectively around Sherri. "It will."

Chapter 13
Child's Play or Baby Love?

Rosemary observed the not-so-new brown Toyota with its California license plate pull in and park somewhat haphazardly in one of the spaces, and watched the two youngsters emerge from the car. *My, they look awfully young to be marrying*, she thought as she nodded her head from side to side.

As Derek and Betty-Sue approached the office, Rosemary managed a closer look. They entered both in their denim trousers and sneakers; she wearing a loose-fitting blouse and he sporting a tee-shirt. Betty-Sue was looking down, as Derek struggled to fill out the forms.

"Just driven up this afternoon, have you?" Rosemary inquired, attempting to engage in small conversation. She was only too well aware of the situation surrounding this wedding, having witnessed so many similar style weddings before. Over the years, she had become exceedingly prescient in recognizing the circumstances of those arriving in her office. In this instance, she was going to have to act quickly, tactfully, and carefully.

Betty-Sue nodded affirmatively. She was a rather plain young lady. *A little pale and mousy looking—definitely timid*, Rosemary thought.

"Actually, we left Pomona, California, this morning. There was just a lot of traffic," Derek expressed dismissively, a slight degree of discomfort in his voice. There was a boyish look about him. He was trying to appear older and more mature than he actually was. They both seemed very nervous, and Rosemary wondered just how many months pregnant the young girl was.

They were barely high school graduates. Derek had planned to continue to college with dreams of becoming an architect. He knew he would have to pay his own way, as his parents were not in a position to afford his tuition. Betty-Sue's parents were not well positioned financially, either. She originally intended to pursue a career in interior design. With the advent of the baby, both of them now had to abandon their dreams and deal with reality.

The teenagers had been raised in Oklahoma to respectable, hard-working, suburban families, although Betty-Sue's parents were considerably stricter. Her father was very stern with her, even though she was his pride and joy, his princess. Having been the closest of friends for years, both families moved to Pomona, California a year earlier. Derek and Betty-Sue were childhood sweethearts and it was always assumed that one day they would marry. Nobody knew it would be so early, while they were still both so young.

"You didn't make an appointment here, did you?" Rosemary continued.

Derek looked a little startled. "I didn't know we needed one."

"Not a problem," Rosemary reassured. "Hope you don't mind waiting, though. There's a service in the chapel in progress, and then there's a break before the next couple. I'm sure we can squeeze you in. Why don't you take a seat?" she offered cheerfully, gesturing to the couch.

Derek sat and started twiddling his thumbs. Betty-Sue sat alongside with eyes still cast downward, her hands clutching her small purse.

There was an uneasy quiet. Buster began playing with his toys behind the counter, biting on a plastic pork chop, trying to resurrect its long lost squeak. He discarded it in favor of his regular dog bone, gnashing and clawing at the remaining morsels of meat.

"Can I pour you both some coffee or water?" Rosemary offered moving toward the coffee pot.

"Yes, please. Just water for me," Betty-Sue said, looking up for the first time.

Derek shook his head. "No thanks."

Rosemary poured the cup and rounded the counter, handing it to Betty-Sue, seating herself on Betty-Sue's other side.

Rosemary touched Betty-Sue's hand gently. "Is something the matter?"

"Nothing, nothing's the matter," she replied, somewhat taken aback. "Why do you ask?"

"Why, it's your wedding day. This should be the happiest day of your life. You're a bride! You don't look very happy to me. In fact, you both look very troubled." She looked at Derek for confirmation.

"We're both fine," he said forcibly. "I'll take care of Betty-Sue."

"Oh, I'm sure you will," Rosemary quickly added, not wishing to offend him. She couldn't afford to alienate him. "But ..."

Betty-Sue didn't allow Rosemary to complete her thought. "I'm going to keep my baby," she interjected.

"Betty-Sue, we agreed we weren't going to tell anybody." Derek angrily jumped up from his seat.

"She knows. She can tell," Betty-Sue replied. She turned back to Rosemary. "Nobody's going to talk me out of it, nor will anyone take my baby away. It's our child, isn't it, Derek?" This was easier than Rosemary thought. In prior experience, it took quite a while to coax this information out of the young would-be mothers when they arrived at the chapel. Even so, she didn't have much time.

"Of course it's your child ... and I'm sure you will make a wonderful mother. Where do you plan on raising your child?" she asked, knowing these two confused children had not thought everything through.

"I'll take care of everything. We're heading north toward Reno and Carson City to find work. If nothing's there, we'll keep going to Idaho. I'll get a job," Derek said defiantly.

Rosemary admired this young, naïve adolescent, so determined to do what was right. He clearly had an old head firmly planted on his very young shoulders. Rosemary pressed further. "Have you checked the job markets? What sort of work will you do?"

Derek shrugged. "I'll do whatever it takes." He tried to appear nonchalant.

"We love each other. That's what matters," Betty-Sue confided.

Rosemary tried to gain their confidence, seeming nonjudgmental. "Of course you love each other. I bet your parents are pleased and happy for you both," she offered gingerly, testing the waters, knowing full well that neither would have told their parents.

Betty-Sue shot back, a flash of horror on her face. "My parents must never find out. My daddy will kill me. Please!" she begged. "You can't contact my parents or Derek's. His mother and father are close friends of my parents. They must never know." She looked panic stricken, turning to Derek for support. "Derek, you didn't have to list daddy's phone number on the forms, did you?" Betty-Sue knew all hell would break loose if her father ever found out. It might have been okay for other parents' kids to get pregnant, but certainly not hers.

Rosemary put her arm further around Betty-Sue's shoulders. "But my dear, you have someone else to consider now. You have your child to think about," she advised gently. "You wouldn't want your baby to grow up never knowing who the grandparents are, would you? You don't want to go through your life without ever speaking to your parents again? I'm sure they love you very much. Can you imagine the hurt and pain they will suffer?" She tried not to make it sound as if she was placing guilt or blame on them. She just wanted them to be sure the decisions they were making were the right ones for them.

"We don't have a choice," Derek argued boldly. "They would never approve of our marriage. They wouldn't understand. *You* don't understand. We **have** to go it alone," he said emphatically.

"But you don't," countered Rosemary in her consoling and understanding manner. "I know you mean well, and you want what is best for your new family. But why would you want to put yourself and your wife-to-be through such stress and anxiety? I know you'll get work somewhere, but what sort of a life will it be? What will you do when the baby's born?" There was a calming influence in Rosemary's voice as she quietly tried to persuade the youths to see reason.

Betty-Sue was beginning to soften. "Maybe she's right, Derek. After all, we only have five hundred dollars," she said meekly.

Derek sat back down next to Betty-Sue and took her hands in his, looking into her eyes. "That's plenty. Remember our plans."

"Five hundred dollars? That will get you nowhere. I implore you to call your parents," Rosemary pleaded. "If not, why don't you let me call them?" She was trying not to be intrusive and nosy, while trying to show her compassion for the confused couple. It was a delicate balance, but one in which she had gained much experience over the years.

Betty-Sue and Derek vacillated as they weighed Rosemary's sage advice. They had told none of their friends and family of their plans. Rosemary was the first and only person with whom they had discussed their predicament. Somehow, they found it easier to talk to Rosemary. Maybe it was because she seemed objective, or because she didn't know any of the friends and family. No matter, they knew she could be trusted.

Sensing she was winning, Rosemary extricated herself briefly from the situation. "Let me take Buster for a short walk, while you sit here and consider your options." She slipped the leash on the collar around Buster's willing neck.

Derek and Betty-Sue pondered Rosemary's offer. They decided they had nothing to lose if Rosemary called the parents. They knew she would not reveal their whereabouts. If the parents were willing to listen, they would go home; if not, they would get married at the chapel and proceed with their plans. It was a win-win situation for them.

"But what if they trace the call? They'll see the area code on the telephone screen," Betty-Sue asked.

"Oh, they won't be able to trace the call," Rosemary said when she returned from her walk with Buster. "I have a blocked telephone number." Betty-Sue and Derek looked relieved. "Whose parents shall I call, and what are their names?" she inquired.

"Mine," Betty-Sue said quietly. "Their first names are Ed and Sally."

Before they could change their minds, Rosemary dialed the number she was given.

"Hello, this is Eddie," came the strong masculine voice over the telephone line.

"Eddie, you don't know me, but my name is Rosemary. I'm sitting next to your daughter Betty-Sue and her boyfriend, Derek."

Eddie sounded alarmed. "Are they all right? Is something the matter?"

"Who is it, dear?" Rosemary heard in the background. She assumed it was Betty-Sue's mother.

"It's a lady by the name of Rosemary. She's with Betty-Sue and Derek."

Sally picked up the extension of telephone. "Is anything wrong?" she asked anxiously.

"Nothing to worry about. They're both fine. No accident or anything," Rosemary assured them. Pleased that she had both parents' attention at the same time, and without even remotely hinting where she was calling from, she proceeded to break the news of Betty-Sue's pregnancy.

"Over my dead body is she going to have a baby!" Ed exploded. "She'll come home and we'll see that the baby is taken care of. She'll have an operation. How dare she disgrace us!" he yelled.

Sally was sobbing. "Is my little girl all right? Why didn't she come to us?"

"Forgive me." Rosemary tried to keep the subject on an even keel. "You heard what your husband said, but Betty-Sue doesn't want an operation. She wants to have the baby. And you know what? I think she is going to make a wonderful little mother, too."

"Maybe later on she will," Ed continued to thunder. "But right now, she will come home at once and take her lumps," he commanded.

Sally continued to cry. "Where is she? Where are you? And who are you?" She struggled to absorb it all.

"Oh, I'm just someone who wants to see the family reunited and the baby born into a loving home with loving parents and loving grandparents. You **are** going to be grandparents, you know," she added slowly for good measure, emphasizing their new roles. "Think about that. There is nothing quite like the miracle of a newborn child. It's a wonderful gift." There was silence on the phone. Ed and Sally were most likely pondering the impact of the news.

Ed softened. "We had such high hopes for our only child. We wanted her to have a big white wedding, a bright future, and someone who would take care of her."

"Oh, I think Derek will take care of her just fine," Rosemary counseled. She was certain of that.

"Can I speak to my baby?" Sally asked, still crushed by the news.

Rosemary put her hand over the mouthpiece. "Betty-Sue, do you want to speak to your parents now?" Betty-Sue nodded and took the telephone. Rosemary kept her arms around her for comfort.

"Mama? Dad?" She started to cry.

"Why didn't you tell us?" her father asked, still somewhat stunned.

"I wanted to. I tried to. I just couldn't. I just couldn't." Betty-Sue sobbed. "I'm so sorry. I'm so sorry. Please forgive me."

"We love you, baby. We'll always love you," her mother intervened.

"Just come home. Please just come home. Where are you, anyway?" Ed asked. Betty-Sue handed the phone back to Rosemary and ran to Derek, who held her tightly in his arms.

Rosemary took the phone again.

"Can you please send them home right now? We'll sort this out and take care of things," said Sally, regaining her composure.

"I think it's been a long day for the young ones. They're in Las Vegas." Rosemary said.

"Las Vegas?" asked Ed. "What in the world are they doing there?"

He was strangely oblivious as to the reason behind Derek and Betty-Sue's being in Sin City. Rosemary was not of the mind to enlighten him. Ed and Sally had had enough of a shock for one day, she decided.

Ignoring his question, she suggested, "It's late afternoon and I don't think they should be making that long drive back to California. You're both in Pomona, right near Ontario airport. You're only an hour's flight away. I know a nice little motel where I can make room reservations for you all if you like. You can be here in a couple of hours and talk things through. Then you can all drive back tomorrow. Why don't you just let me check the motel availability, and we'll call you back?" It was more of a gentle command, couched as a suggestion. Ed and Sally both thought it was a good idea and hung up.

Rosemary's strategy worked. She turned to Derek and Betty-Sue, explaining her plan. "It will be good that you'll be meeting on neutral ground. By the time they get here, the shock will have worn off. Hopefully you will able to discuss things calmly."

"But what if they don't?" Derek started to panic. "What if …?"

"Then you just pack your bags and jump in the car and come over to my house. It's small, but there will be a bed for you for the night. They won't have a car so they can't follow you. I doubt that is going to happen. Your mother and father sound like lovely, good people, Betty-Sue. They're over the initial shock and heartache. They'll see things your way," Rosemary concluded.

Rosemary dialed the motel and booked two rooms. She knew the motel owner, explained the situation, and assured her that even though there was no credit card, she would have no trouble getting the payment when the guests arrived. Rosemary was certain of it. Having also experienced similar situations, her friend understood perfectly. She also trusted

Rosemary's judgment. Rosemary had Derek call Ed and Sally and give them the motel information. She thought it would be good for them to break the ice over the telephone.

Then Rosemary ushered them out of the office, giving them directions to the motel as they walked.

"How can we ever thank you?" Betty-Sue asked gratefully. "I don't know how we can repay you."

"Maybe you can come to our wedding?" Derek offered, already looking relieved at the turn of events.

"I'd like that," Rosemary smiled.

For Derek, the worst was over. He was not concerned about telling his parents. They were more modern in their thinking and more pragmatic. Sure, they would be upset, but he knew they would deal with it. It was the relationship with Betty-Sue and her parents that had always worried him.

They both gave Rosemary a big hug before getting in their car. "If the baby is a girl, I'm going to call her Rosemary," Betty-Sue said impulsively, but genuinely.

Rosemary beamed; her eyes started to glisten. She waved as the young couple drove off.

Chapter 14
A Model of a Marriage

As Rosemary turned toward the office, two minivans sporting local news television station logos on their side panels simultaneously swerved into the chapel parking lot entrance, almost running her over. She was immediately suspicious. She hurriedly ran into the office and reviewed her appointment book to see who would be arriving next, fearing it might be some celebrity. She loathed celebrity weddings. The media, in her opinion, showed such little respect for the bride and groom and for the solemnity of the occasion. She viewed them with total disdain believing they had no respect nor regard for other people's property. In particular, they trampled on her precious flowering shrubs and bushes, which irked her.

The names "Peter and Renee" were written in the appointment book. No last name, nothing more. Not even a telephone number. *Hmmm*, she thought. *I wonder who that can be*. The names did not register with her at all. Nonetheless, she sensed the inevitable, hearing more cars entering the site. She looked out the office window and viewed five vans from the media. Numerous people were now positioning themselves, some holding cameras and others clutching microphones. She recognized some reporters from the nightly television news.

As she had done so many times before during celebrity weddings, she slipped outside the back door of the office and sneaked into the chapel via the rear entrance. Tiptoeing along the aisle, she quietly closed the two main doors to the chapel, locking them from the inside with the bolt. She latched the back door of the chapel, returned to the office and closed the front door to keep Buster inside.

She heard the soft and gentle purr of a vehicle pulling into the driveway, halting close to the office entrance. Out stepped Peter, who offered his hand to assist Renee out of the luxurious limousine. There was an immediate onslaught of photographers clicking away, light bulbs flashing from the multitude of cameras. A mass of reporters surged forward with their microphones.

"Where are you spending your honeymoon?"

"Do you plan on having a family?"

"Will you continue to live in Las Vegas?" they all demanded.

Peter was furious that someone had obviously leaked the news of their wedding. Only a few people knew. However, he was not about to let it spoil Renee's special day. He protectively put his arms around her and helped her up the stairs into the office. As soon as they entered, Rosemary closed and locked the door behind them.

"Worse than vultures!" she said disdainfully. "I can assure you, your wedding will be private. I have locked the main entrance to the chapel."

Peter was relieved. "Thank you," he said gratefully.

"Your concern and consideration is much appreciated," Renee declared in her soft, sultry voice. Rosemary now recognized the very elegant and beautiful Renee standing in front of her. Her face had been on the cover of so many magazines, and her television advertisements promoting her own perfume, REPENT, were well known to even the most casual television audience viewer. Who had not heard the commercial—"Feeling wicked?" came the taunting voice. "Then buy REPENT." The advertisement showed Renee holding the bottle of perfume, and in her distinctive and seductive voice, lured the viewer into buying it.

Renee looked every bit the glamorous model on her wedding day, in her long, traditional, white satin dress. Peter appeared remarkably dapper in his black tuxedo. Fortunately, it was late in the afternoon, and the weather was comfortable and cool.

"My, you do make a handsome couple," complimented Rosemary.

"I'm the luckiest man alive," said Peter. "You look so beautiful," he gazed adoringly at his soon-to-be wife. He began to think back to the day they first met, three short years almost to the day. How much his life had changed since that fateful morning.

He had been summoned to jury duty and was late. He ran across the street to the federal court building and as he approached the entrance, he stomped out his cigarette butt under his shoe. Fortunately, there was not a long line passing through the security check. There were a few people already waiting in the jury pool room, but still, he was not the last to arrive. He heaved a sigh of relief and poured himself some coffee from the coffeemaker in the small self-serve cafeteria. He returned to the jury room and waited impatiently for the instructions. He was hoping to be dismissed. It would be a huge inconvenience for him otherwise.

Peter was one of many professional photographers in Las Vegas, having his own studio not far from the strip. It was not the most successful studio, but he was freelance, and made a living that at least paid his bills. Most of his work was referral from satisfied local clients. He was successful mainly photographing family portraits, weddings, graduations, and other special events. Occasionally he managed a commercial photo shoot. He felt he should receive more, but even with all his contacts in the advertising world, he somehow never had a real major break.

As he looked out the window into the small atrium, where smokers were allowed to indulge, he saw Renee exhaling smoke from a cigarette. He caught the alluring angle of her head as she stood partly in the shadows and partly in the sunshine. *What a stunning beauty*, Peter thought. *What a unique look she has. This could be the model I've been waiting for.* He scooped up his polystyrene cup of coffee and hastened to the small atrium, hoping she was not already modeling with an agency.

He lit a cigarette, engaging in small talk about the aggravation of being called for jury service. Renee was ambivalent about being asked to serve. She was a showgirl in one of the glitzy Vegas revue shows on the strip, working nights. It made no difference to her if she had to sit in a courtroom during the day for a short while.

"I just knew your career had to be in the world of glamour," Peter said a little audaciously. "Have you ever considered a career in modeling?" Peter was not handsome, but he had a cute, boyish smile that Renee found quite charming. He was … well … cute, she thought. She tossed her head back and laughed.

"Heavens no! I don't have what it takes for that." She was all too well aware of how many stunningly beautiful women there were, especially in Sin City. She worked with enough of them in the chorus line. In her earlier career, she had been a beautician demonstrating cosmetics at one of the top department stores in Vegas, before being hired as makeup consultant for the revue show in which she now appeared. She knew all about aspiring models.

"That's where you're wrong," Peter said, knowing that his photographs of her could turn her into an instant phenomenon. They were both suddenly summoned to the jury room. "Please call me, and let's spend a day at my studio. No charge. What do you have to lose?" he suggested, handing her his business card.

What did she have to lose? she pondered.

When she was called to serve on the jury, she noticed that Peter was not among the jurors. He had been dismissed with the thanks of the court. That night she spoke to Desiree, the showgirl who occupied the makeup booth next to hers.

"Hey, Desiree, does that boyfriend of yours still do private eye work? Could you have him check out this photographer for me?"

A week later, Desiree came back with the answer Renee hoped for. "Clean as a whistle, honey. No record. No bad debts. No trouble with the law. This one could qualify for sainthood. What's the deal? Anyway, it's on the house, sugar."

After the show that night, Renee was alone in her apartment. Peter's offer kept recurring in her mind. She thought back to her teenage years growing up in Southern California, remembering her summer jobs when she was employed at the little perfume store in Orleans Square in Disneyland. The perfumery allowed women to blend the various fragrances, enabling them to bottle their own unique perfume. While working there, she accidentally stumbled upon a formula that she knew would be a sure fire winner. It had been her dream to launch and market her own perfume one day. What had happened to her dreams, she wondered? Peter gave her confidence and had faith in her. If he could do something with the photographs, maybe she could fulfill her dream. It was a long shot, but the next day, she called Peter and scheduled to see him the following Monday.

Peter was excited. He told her to have several changes of clothing, and he would pick her up at nine o'clock.

A stickler for punctuality, he was at her door at the appointed time. She was amazed at the amount of photographic equipment in the back seat of his car, and wondered why it wasn't all in his studio.

Peter explained that they were heading up to Mount Charleston before the sun was too high in the sky. He wanted some shots of her surrounded by the pine trees and the snow, with the sun glistening. As they drove up the winding road, the beautiful bright blue sky was penetrating through the trees. There was not a cloud in sight.

"It's a perfect day for a photo shoot," Peter said, as he parked the car and gathered his equipment. She showed remarkable patience while he constantly clicked his cameras.

"Look seductive. Look happy. Look sultry. Head up. Be pensive," he ordered. *She was a natural*, he thought. *How could she have gone unnoticed all these years? I have a Princess Grace in the making*, he imagined. He had her change clothes in the lodge at the top of the mountain, and once again, he commanded her. "Where's the smile? Let me see carefree. Give me demure." She looked comfortable and at ease. He snapped color shots, zoom shots, black and white, using a myriad of soft focus lenses.

After Mount Charleston, they headed off to the beautiful and majestic Valley of Fire State Park with its rich, deep red rock formations. The sky was a perfect blue, and the combination created magnificent backdrops. Once again, Peter clicked away, asking her to change her clothes yet again in the visitor center. He also had brought along some props. He handed her assorted pastel shaded and solid scarves for her to drape over her shoulders, slightly mask her face, and to tie her long wavy hair in a pony tail.

At the end of the photo shoot in the park, he surprised her by opening his car trunk and bringing out a blanket and a picnic basket. He had packed a delicious meal of assorted pates, gourmet cheeses and crackers, grapes, and a couple of chilled bottles of wine. She was moved by the romance of the moment. She had not detected such sentimental thoughtfulness in this man. He was turning out to be quite a charmer. "May as well have some pleasure with the business," he grinned.

After the picnic, they drove back to his studio for more pictures.

"Now I know how Princess Diana felt," Renee laughed as Peter continued to flash away.

His studio was scantily furnished with the minimum of necessities for a business to function. The desk was scattered with papers and sticky notes and a red light flashed on his answering machine. He ignored the flashing signals and concentrated on his prize find. He couldn't wait to take these pictures to his colleagues in the advertising agencies.

"Why are you doing this, and what's in it for you?" Renee asked curiously as they enjoyed dinner that night at his favorite sushi restaurant.

"If anything comes from this, as I think it will," Peter retorted, playing with his chopsticks, "in any commercial contract, you make it a condition that I alone will have the sole rights to photographing you."

"It's a deal," she laughed, extending her hand for a handshake, confident that nothing would come to pass.

"And what will you do with all the money when I make you rich and famous?" he toyed.

She shared with him her dream of launching her own brand of perfume.

"I'll be your business manager. After all, I did major in business and economics in college," he said, half joking.

"Then you've really got yourself a deal." Renee raised her wine glass as if to toast.

"Have you thought of a name for your brand of perfume?" Peter wondered aloud. Renee had given the subject much thought but had yet to come up with a name. "How about REPENT?" he suggested. "It has all the letters from your name, and all the letters from mine."

"How very clever. I like it. REPENT it is." Renee marveled at his creativity.

"Here's to us," Peter toasted, clinking his glass with hers.

He feverishly put together a marketable photographic portfolio of his protégé, still amazed that she had never modeled before. He was ecstatic he had managed to capture in his photos what first attracted him to her when they met at the courthouse. He set about visiting his friends and colleagues at the various agencies and magazines, pushing her portfolio. Within days, he managed to land a fairly lucrative contract promoting elegant furs in the print media, followed by further advertisements for exclusive leather handbags. She was well on her way, when she was approached to market diamonds and jewelry in television still shots.

True to her word, she ensured that Peter had sole photography rights, and he disappointed no one. Soon, demands for her face came pouring in from all over. Peter surrendered his studio and devoted his entire career to managing hers. He was surprisingly good at it, managing the contracts and all the finances adroitly. He became her manager, her mentor, her protector, her best friend, and finally … her lover. She had never been happier, and thrived on the attention and love that Peter gave to her.

Eventually, enough capital was set aside to start her perfume business. It was arduous starting up the business venture and partnership, but it became the dream for both of them, and Peter was determined to make their dream a reality. As Renee became a household name, Peter did not mind working behind the scenes, and they were soon ready to launch the product. They first marketed REPENT in the United States to see how it sold. Renee advertised it extensively in magazines and on television. The product took off like a rocket, and Renee and Peter moved into the much sought-after luxury complex of Turnberry Place just off the Las Vegas Strip, reveling in the fame and fortune.

They were now on the verge of marketing REPENT

internationally, and planned on flying to London, Paris, and Rome to start a worldwide promotion.

"Peter, before we leave for Europe, why don't we get married?" she asked spontaneously.

"I'm supposed to ask that question," Peter said flatly, slightly embarrassed. He had focused so much on the dream he had failed to recognize the obvious.

They decided on a very small and private wedding at The Chapel of Eternal Love, the day before they left for Europe, which would be part work, part honeymoon.

As they gazed lovingly into each other's eyes at the chapel, the press were still pounding forcibly on the portal of the office. Buster barked loudly in return, annoyed at their constant harassment.

"Come on," said Rosemary. She pressed the buzzer under the counter to alert the minister, using a special code to let him know it was a celebrity wedding and the participants would be coming through the rear door. Once they were safey inside the chapel, she locked the door behind them, and returned to the front office.

Rosemary hoped that the press would go away. About twenty minutes later, she heard the back door of the chapel open, and Peter and Renee hurried back into her office. They were both beaming that their solemn and special day had not been ruined by the media. They had Rosemary to thank for that. After hugging her profusely, Renee removed a little bottle of REPENT from her small handbag and handed it to Rosemary.

"I do hope you like it," Renee offered. "And I thank you from the bottom of my heart."

The Chapel of Eternal Love

Rosemary was touched. She would never have been able to afford such an exquisite item. As she quietly tried to open the front door, Renee and Peter dashed to their limousine through the flashing of cameras and the horde of paparazzi yelling and screaming.

Rosemary closed the door and sat down behind her desk. She opened the bottle and dabbed a drop on both her wrists. *Oh, what a heavenly fragrance.* She leaned over to pat Buster, who responded with a series of sneezes. He was totally unfamiliar with the aroma.

She watched the limo slowly back out of the parking lot, followed by all the cars with their television logos on the side. *Thank goodness*, she sighed, as she pondered the lives of luxury and glamour, the world in which Peter and Renee moved. She clutched her bottle of REPENT and rocked back and forth in her chair, wondering who would be coming to the chapel next.

Chapter 15
Love Reunited

Linh took her seat at the back of the class. She had enrolled in a night course at the College of Southern Nevada in English as a Second Language. Not that she really needed it. She had mastered the language when she first moved to America fifteen years earlier and was extremely proficient. Besides, she only intended to attend a couple of the lessons. She had an ulterior motive for being there.

When she was a mere twenty-years-old, Linh arrived in America from Vietnam to study in California. Being timid and shy by nature, it was hard to leave her mother and her familiar surroundings and venture to a new world and way of life. For her entire young life it had always been just the two of them—mother and daughter. Now she was alone. During her first years in America, it was strange for Linh to adopt the culture of her new country, and she yearned for her simple life in the quiet suburbs of Ho Chi Minh City.

Many a night she cried herself to sleep in her shared apartment off campus in Los Angeles, but she had a compelling reason for staying in America. She was determined to find the American father who had deserted her before she was even born. Linh had seen the only picture of her father that her mother had and knew only what her mother had told her about him.

"He was the only man I ever loved. He was strong, handsome, and kind. He wanted so much for the two of us to be in a different time and place—in a different world. I know he loved me," she repeated every time the subject came up.

Like many wartime relationships, Kim-Ly and her American GI boyfriend, Phil, were separated by circumstances beyond their control. As Saigon was falling, Kim-Ly fled the city and across the fields to the village where her grandmother lived and where she hoped she would be safe. Kim-Ly stayed away from the chaos and devastation of the city and gave birth to her daughter, Linh, in the quiet of the countryside. When Americans withdrew from Vietnam, Phil's service was brought abruptly to an end, and he was sent back to the US on short and hurried notice. He tried to contact Kim-Ly before leaving, but to no avail. The fates had conspired against them.

When her grandmother died, Kim-Ly returned to the city and took a job as a nurse at the hospital. Linh was five years old. Kim-Ly was capable and knowledgeable, and over the years became the chief nurse in the hospital. She had a strong and caring nature but nothing matched the love she had for her daughter. Linh was her only link with her American G.I. hero, Phil. She set aside money from her pay to ensure that her daughter would be able to travel to America for a fine college education and see the land of her father's birth.

Linh completed her four years at California State University and moved to San Francisco, where she was hired by the Vietnamese Consulate. It was Linh's ambition to become a diplomat, possibly in the United Nations, but she knew that would be a while. By working at the Consulate in San Francisco, she was allowed to remain in the United

States, despite the expiration of her student visa. This enabled her to hire a detective and pursue her other dream of finding her father.

She provided the private investigator with the very few details she had. Just her father's name, a copy of his photograph, and that he lived somewhere in California in the early 1970s. She called the detective periodically for updates, but it was always the same. He drew blanks along every avenue.

Finally, he called Linh with the information she had been waiting so long to hear. He had tracked Phil down in Las Vegas, teaching. For all the years she had been waiting, she was now confused and in a turmoil. Should she call her mother? Should she call her father? Her *father*? She actually had a father who was living. It was almost unthinkable. At thirty-five-years-old, she learned she had a father. She had planned what she was going to say and do for years, but now that the time was here, she abandoned all her carefully made plans as the raw emotion of the situation overcame her. Her heart pounded furiously.

She dropped the phone from the detective without inquiring what path he took that led him to locate Phil. It didn't matter. She felt excited and afraid ... and angry. Why did she have to track *him* down? Why couldn't he have located *her*? What if he didn't acknowledge her as his daughter? She was happy that at least this long-awaited chapter that had consumed so much of her life would now have an ending, and hopefully a new beginning. All these thoughts and feelings churned through her mind and body.

She decided not to let her mother know until she had a few more questions answered. Maybe Phil was married and had another life and family. With his good looks, Linh thought for sure this would be the case.

She went online and enrolled in her father's class that was starting the following week. She asked for and received two weeks leave from her supervisor, packed a couple of suitcases, and headed for Sin City. After a friend drove her to the airport and a short flight, she arrived in Las Vegas, rented a car, and checked in at the Extended Stays Inn. The accommodation was functional and within her budget.

Soon, she was sitting in the class like a nervous little schoolgirl, awaiting the arrival of her teacher ... her father. There was noise and hubbub around her as the other students were chattering, but she paid no attention. Her heart was beating and throbbing so loudly, she thought the whole class could hear.

"Good evening, everyone," boomed a voice, dominating the classroom. She stared as he entered the room and headed straight to the teacher's desk. "I will be your instructor for this semester, and I would like to start by everyone introducing themselves and explaining why you are here," he continued.

Linh focused her eyes on him. He was a little taller than she imagined. His dashing good looks had not faded with time, his rugged jaw line just as it was in the photograph. She didn't hear the other class attendees introduce themselves. The sound was a blur. After she heard the lady in front of her say her name, Linh tried to stand up to introduce herself. Her legs and body trembled.

"My name is Linh, and I am here to learn," she said weakly but firmly.

Phil's face turned pale. *My God, she looks the image of Kim-*

Ly. He stared at her with a confused and quizzical expression. It was both eerie and uncanny. She had the same svelte figure, short black hair, and large brown eyes on a soft and gentle face. Unnerved, he struggled through the hour-long class. Obviously it could not be Kim-Ly. But he couldn't keep from glancing in Linh's direction as she sat and stared back motionless. She was way too young to be Kim-Ly's age, he tried to justify. Yet he felt a bond with this young lady. He didn't know why.

The class finished and everyone headed for the door to leave. Everyone except for Linh, who felt like she was glued to her chair. Phil awkwardly headed toward the desk where Linh was seated and perched himself on the edge of the desk in front.

"And where are you from, Linh?" he inquired apprehensively.

"I have just moved here from San Francisco. But originally I came from Vietnam," she offered gingerly.

"Linh. That's a pretty Vietnamese name. What does it mean in English?" He was stiff and uncomfortable.

"In English, it mean 'Gentle Spirit'. Have you been to Vietnam?" On the plane, Linh had rehearsed how she was going to handle the situation after seeing Phil in the class, but it wasn't coming out how she planned. She would have to use all the diplomatic skills she had learned at the university so as not to drop a bombshell without preparing her father first.

"I was there during the war. It was a tough time." There was silence. He cast his eyes down. "It is a beautiful country, and I *do* have some beautiful memories, despite it being wartime," he continued, trying to break the ice, and wondering all the while, why he was staying behind at the end of class with this lady. Linh remained silent.

"In fact, you remind me very much of someone I met in Saigon whom I loved very much."

"Would her name be Kim-Ly?" Linh asked, seizing the moment, ignoring his referring to Ho Chi Minh City as Saigon.

Phil became a little concerned about the direction of the conversation. He needed time to think. He deflected the subject of the conversation.

"Say, how about we go for coffee somewhere?" he inquired haltingly and nervously. Linh nodded.

She followed his car and as she was driving, she wondered whether she should reveal who she was. Would it be too soon? Maybe she should wait until the next class. But then, maybe he wouldn't ask her for coffee again?

Once they were settled and had ordered from the waitress, Phil was ready to pursue the line of conversation, although his mind was in turmoil.

"Kim-Ly? That name means Golden-Lion, doesn't it?" he ventured.

"Yes." Linh nodded again. "It is also the name of my mother."

Phil stared in disbelief.

"What was your father's name?" he asked with a great deal of trepidation. He wanted to hear what she had to say, yet he already knew the answer. He knew intuitively. He had felt a bond the first time he laid eyes upon Linh in the classroom.

Linh lowered her eyes. She thought for a moment and then looked up and straight at him. "I believe," she stumbled,

"I believe *you* are my father," she said slowly and deliberately.

"Oh my God! Oh my God!" Phil responded, bewildered, but overjoyed. He jumped out of his seat with outstretched arms. Linh rose and ran to him, and they hugged each other almost desperately. He held her tightly for what seemed an eternity. How she had waited for this moment. To finally feel the arms of her father surround her.

"However did you find me? Why didn't you tell me? How is your mother? Where is your mother? Why didn't you call me?" Question upon question tumbled from his mouth.

She had plenty of questions of her own. But in her quiet demeanor, she allowed him to continue, knowing that she would be able to have her questions answered in due course.

They chatted in the restaurant until dawn.

"Why did you not come back for us?" Linh asked, when she was finally given the chance to ask the one question that had always haunted her.

"I did come back. When the war finished and I could go back, I did. Your mother was not at the same home I visited when I was there. No one knew where she was. It was impossible to find her. And you—I never knew Kim-Ly was carrying my child. I never stopped loving your mother, you know." He opened his wallet. Inside was a faded photograph of Kim-Ly. He showed it to Linh. "I've never stopped carrying this."

"You never married?" Linh asked.

"Never did. I always loved your mother. We have to call your mother. Let's call your mother."

"No!" Linh begged. "Let me do it. Let me prepare her, as I know it will be a shock to her that I have found you. After that, we will both call her."

"Maybe it is not too late to be a family. Maybe your mother would come and live in America?"

"Maybe. Maybe, you could come and live in Vietnam."

They parted as the sun rose above the horizon.

Linh called her mother and gradually but gently broke the news to her. "He's as handsome as he is in your photo. He still loves you. He wants you to come to America, where we can all be a family."

Kim-Ly wept uncontrollably. Linh wished she was there to put her arms around her mother.

Both Phil and Kim-Ly still seemed to be in love with each other. But were they in love with a memory? Was it the time and the place that they were in love with? Maybe time and distance had changed them.

After Phil spoke with Kim-Ly over the phone, he was convinced that the torch he had been carrying had not been in vain. But they were cautious.

Phil offered to fly Kim-Ly to San Francisco, where she could stay with her daughter. Then they would fly to Las Vegas. Phil thought it appropriate that they both stay in a hotel and made the reservations, footing the bill, of course.

He was in communication with Linh every day, and they bonded very quickly. He decided to have a wonderful dinner for his 'Gentle Spirit" and 'Golden Lion' at his home the night they arrived.

He waited patiently at the airport for them to come down the escalator and into the baggage claim area, pacing up and down. *I feel like an expectant father*, he said to himself. *Silly me. I'm thirty-five years too late for that.*

Kim-Ly and Linh finally arrived. The tears were plentiful

as were the hugs and kisses. They all laughed and wept tears of joy. In Phil's eyes, Kim-Ly was as beautiful as ever.

He drove them to their hotel and told them that a limousine would come and bring them to his house that night. Then he went home and prepared a simple but elegant dinner of poached salmon with rice and asparagus. It was light and delicate, he thought. He heard the limousine pull up.

The driver opened the rear door and Kim-Ly stepped out. She looked stunning. Linh didn't follow.

"Why aren't you coming out?" Phil peered into the limousine.

"I think you and Mother should spend this first night alone, Dad," she said. Linh was in heaven. She loved being able to say the word "Dad." She hoped that her parents would pick up the same love and happiness they had discovered all those years ago in far-off, war-torn Vietnam, and prayed they would be a family.

In a way, Phil was disappointed that Linh would not be joining them. But he understood what she was trying to do. He was grateful for that.

It did not take them an evening to rediscover their passionate youth. Phil was insistent that they become a family, and the sooner the better. They had already wasted too much time.

But there was Linh's future to think of. And could Kim-Ly really uproot from the land she knew and just move to America? Phil knew he could live anywhere and teach anywhere, now that he had Kim-Ly and Linh in his life.

All those questions could be dealt with later. They were secondary and unimportant. The first thing was to get married.

He was insistent on that. Kim-Ly and Linh filled a void in his life, of which he was unaware, until they both arrived.

He booked the appointment at the Chapel of Eternal Love, having met and known Rosemary through mutual friends.

Rosemary was delighted for Phil, and ran out to greet the party when they arrived in the limousine. Buster followed, barking profusely.

"Rosemary, please meet my beautiful wife, Golden Lion, and my equally beautiful daughter, Gentle Spirit," he said proudly.

Rosemary embraced them both warmly, before giving Phil a hug.

"I know you will all be so very happy," she said with much joy in her voice. "I just know it."

Phil put one arm around Linh and the other around Kim-Ly.

Buster continued to bark, his tail wagging back and forth, as they all headed toward the office.

Chapter 16
Full Circle

Mitch was desperate for a drink. It was the night before his wedding, and his emotions and demons were playing tricks. He picked up his cars keys several times to make his way to the liquor store for a bottle of scotch. It would help him sleep, or at least get through the night. But every time he made a move he tried to focus on what he had learned from the Alcoholics Anonymous meetings he'd attended over the last two years. He knew in his heart of hearts that one drink and his whole world could fall apart, just as it did when he starting to drink heavily four years ago.

Mitch was a good-looking man in his mid twenties who had everything going for him when he met and married Diana five years earlier. They were made for each other. He was the assistant manager at a large retail department store in what was one of the largest in a national chain. Diana was a stay-at-home housewife, extremely domesticated, who loved cooking and entertaining. They rented a beautiful modest home in the Hollywood Hills in California, where they hoped to raise a large family.

Mitch often called Diana from work late afternoon. "Honey, would you mind if Barry joins us for dinner tonight?"

"Sure," she always said. Barry had been Mitch's best friend since childhood and had been Mitch's best man at their wedding.

Growing up, the two were inseparable, double-dating through high school and college. Even now, they still had boys' night out and attended a sports event together one night a week—either baseball, basketball, football or ice hockey—depending on the season. They were both sports addicts. Diana did not mind their evenings out, though, or Barry's constant weekend visits. She was fond of Barry and the feeling was reciprocated.

"I just wish I could meet someone like you to make my life perfect," Barry joked, every time giving her his customary hug.

"You will. Just be patient," Diana always replied.

True enough, almost a year to the day of Mitch and Diana's wedding Barry brought his new girlfriend, Margot, over to dinner to meet them. She was the latest in a line of dates, but somehow she was different. The evening was a huge success as they all ate, drank, and laughed until the wee hours of the morning. Margot seemed to fit in; it was as if they had all known each other their entire lives.

"Margot's gorgeous, don't you think? And a perfect match for Barry," Diana inquired as she asked Mitch to undo the back of her dress.

"Margot may be hot, but she's not as stunning or as sexy as you." He threw her on the bed and kissed her gently on the cheeks. They were so much in love. Even so, he admitted to himself, if not to Diana, Margot was definitely desirable.

Six months later, Barry and Margot made it down the aisle, with Mitch as best man and Diana as maid of honor.

Mitch and Barry continued to enjoy their sports evenings out, while Diana and Margot either shopped at the mall, went to the movies, or just dined at home—normally at Diana's, since she enjoyed cooking.

One night the two wives were at home, while Diana rustled together a pasta dinner at a moment's notice.

"I admire you for that, Diana," said Margot. "I am hopeless at anything domestic. I don't know why Barry puts up with it. He does most of the cooking in our house. Try as I might, my dishes never seem to come out as planned. I'm just hopeless when it comes to anything culinary."

"He loves you, Margot. That's all that counts."

"We have that in common, Diana. We both have husbands who truly love us. Speaking for myself, I've never been happier."

"Me neither," confided Diana, feeling that she and Mitch were so fortunate to be so much in love. The two women clinked their wine glasses in a toast.

Barry called Mitch. "I have to go Sacramento on an overnight trip tomorrow. Can you and Diana keep an eye on Margot for the night? Maybe have her join you for dinner? I sure hate for her to be alone."

"No problem. We'd love to have her over. I'll speak to Diana when I get home."

When he told Diana of his conversation with Barry, she said, "Oh, honey. I'm going to spend the night with Mum and Dad tomorrow. Did you forget?"

The next day, Mitch called Margot at work. "Look's like it will just be the two of us for dinner. Diana's away, too. What say we go to Yamashiros for Japanese? I can pick you up at seven."

"Sounds good. I love the view from that place. See you then," said Margot.

It was a perfect evening. The sun was setting, and the restaurant, nestled high in the Hollywood Hills, overlooked a myriad of lights that were beginning to glow and twinkle over the vast, sprawling metropolis of Los Angeles.

"I'd almost forgotten how romantic this restaurant is," said Mitch, as they raised their glasses of champagne in a toast.

"Are we celebrating an anniversary or special occasion this evening?" The waiter asked as he removed the dinner plates.

"No. Just friendship," said Mitch. Margot laughed, slightly uncomfortably.

After dinner, Mitch drove Margot back to her home. *God, she looks stunning tonight,* he thought. It was the first time the two of them had ever been alone together.

"Fancy a nightcap?"

Mitch nodded affirmatively, wondering whether it was quite the right thing.

Margot poured them both a brandy and put on some soft background music. Mitch took Margot's hand and gently pulled her toward him, and they started dancing slowly to the rhythm of the music. They both sensed something forbidden was about to take place, but neither was about to stop it. They looked into each other's eyes, then without saying a word, Mitch gently picked Margot up and carried her into the bedroom, closing the door behind him with a kick of his shoe.

Barry was elated that his business concluded early. His

presentation went well and was an easier sell than he thought. He might just be able to catch the last flight to Burbank and be home to surprise Margot. He knew how she loved surprises. He would probably be there before she got home from Mitch and Diana's.

He was startled to see his friend's car in the driveway, blocking his entry into the garage. He parked on the street, and quietly unlocked the front door to the house. He was mystified as to why no one was in the living room. He heard the music playing and saw the two brandy snifters on the coffee table. He felt a little uneasy and puzzled as he walked into the kitchen and dining room, discovering no one. Finally, he opened the bedroom door and saw his best friend Mitch and his wife Margot in his bed.

"Oh my God!" he yelled. He turned and ran into the living room, putting his head in his hands, sobbing in disbelief. How could this have happened? Margot hurriedly appeared in the living room, wrapping a gown around her. "Barry, Barry!" she pleaded.

"Shut up, you whore," he screamed. "Just shut up! Don't say a word to me! Where's that bastard?" He got up and turned to go back into the bedroom just as Mitch came out. "Damn you, you son of a bitch! Damn you!" he hollered and lunged a punch at Mitch. "Get the hell out of my house, you hear? Just get the hell out. I never want to see you again, you bastard!"

Mitch left and drove home, relieved that Diana would not be there. How in the world was he going to explain to her what had happened—what he had done? He poured himself a drink ,which he drank in one gulp, and then poured a couple of others, finally passing out on the couch in a drunken stupor.

Diana returned home mid morning the next day to find her husband still asleep on the couch. She was bewildered. What was he doing at home? Why wasn't he at work? She went to shake him, and noticed the bruise on his chin. What on earth had happened?

Mitch stirred and sat up, feeling his head. He had a splitting headache. "Let me make us some coffee," said Diana anxiously, "so you can tell me what has happened." The realization of what had happened was already resurfacing in Mitch's mind.

She sat on the chair across from him on the couch and listened in utter disbelief as he relayed the events of the previous evening. He saw the ashen, hurt, and pained look on her face.

"Honey, please forgive me. I love you. It was a mistake." Mitch went toward her, moving to put his arms around her and comfort her.

Diana rose to her feet. She looked him straight in the eyes and raised a hand. With all her might, she slapped him across the face as hard as she could. "Don't you touch me! Don't you dare touch me!" she threatened, her voice trembling with rage. "I'm going home to Mother's. Tomorrow I will file for divorce. I never want to hear from you or see you again. Just stay out of my life. Do you hear me?" She grabbed her purse, wiped her eyes from the tears that were now streaming down her face, and ran from the house.

Mitch's world crashed. He had lost his wife whom he loved, and his best friend of twenty years, all through one stupid mistake, a reckless act of lust and passion. He hoped that given time, either Diana or Barry would forgive him. The weeks went by, and then months. He turned more and more to alcohol for comfort and solace, hoping it would rid him of his guilt. Eventually, it interfered with his work. He was called into the manager's office and threatened with three months probation.

He knew he had to start a new life, and admitted to his drinking problem. He explained that he had lost his wife and his best friend, though without going into any specific detail.

His boss was sympathetic. "We have a new location opening in Las Vegas. I can recommend you, but you will have to do something about your drinking problem."

"I will," said Mitch. "I'll try."

"You'll have to do better than that, young man. You'll have to promise me that you'll go to Alcoholics Anonymous meetings in Las Vegas. We have invested a lot in you, and you have a lot of potential."

Mitch accepted the offer and the challenge and moved to Las Vegas. He attended AA meetings, first going three times a week and then cutting it back to twice. He didn't date at all. Truth was, he was still in love with Diana. He threw himself into his new job. Because it was a new store it took a lot of organization and he put in a great deal of overtime. He now supervised ten department heads.

With Christmas coming, his staff chipped in together and purchased him a "Gentleman's Grooming" gift certificate at one of the luxurious spas on the Las Vegas strip. It included a facial, a manicure, a pedicure, and a massage. He was not particularly keen on body treatments, but to appease his staff, he had no other choice.

He booked an afternoon appointment for a hand, feet and face treatment, which he enjoyed more than he thought.

Feeling relaxed, he was ready for the body massage. The lady attendant directed him to his room, and told him to lay on the table with the towel round his waist and wait for the masseuse. He closed his eyes and lay face down, listening to the rippling new age music playing softly in the background. He felt at peace and at ease. He barely heard the door open, but recognized the voice immediately.

"And how are we doing today?"

What in the world was Diana doing here? He spun around.

"Oh God, no. It's you!" She turned to leave.

"No wait. Please stay!" Mitch pleaded and hurried to the door, blocking it before she could leave.

She looked at him. He still had that same handsome face. Over the years since the divorce, her anger had dissipated. Deep down she knew she still loved him. She had never remarried. Nor had she found anyone as attractive as Mitch.

"I can't deal with this, Mitch. I'll have to get someone else to do your massage."

"Can I at least call you? Please. Please let me at least call you," he begged.

She nodded, but brushed him aside, and left to arrange a replacement.

Mitch called her the next day at work, encouraged by her willingness to at least speak to him. Did he have a chance of winning her back?

"You can't call me here at work," Diana said sternly. "Call me at home. Here's my number."

He called her that night, and with a mixed emotion of trepidation and apprehension, she agreed to meet him for dinner. She insisted they meet at the restaurant. The conversation was not easy. He wondered how she came to Las Vegas and how she became a masseuse.

"As you know, I had no marketable skills. After we split, I went to night school and learned to become a masseuse. The instructor said I had excellent healing hands. I found a job, but needed to get away from LA. I came here for a weekend with a friend, and we treated ourselves to a massage where I am now working. It's classy, elegant, with a good respectable clientele. I do well for myself."

"I'm proud of you, Diana. You've done great for yourself, and you look fantastic. But then you always did."

Charming as ever, she thought. *Certain things don't change.* However, she was not about to let him sweet talk her. Not yet anyway. He had a long road to walk before that could happen. She shrugged. "And how did you land in Las Vegas? Do you live here or are you visiting?"

Mitch relayed how his life took a real downhill turn after their marriage ended, how he became an alcoholic and it almost cost him his job. He was finally getting his life back on track.

"My life would be better if I had you back in it," he said. "I know I don't deserve it, but would you at least consider giving me another chance?" He reached across the table.

"Let's see how things go. I'm not making any promises." She kept her arms and hands in her lap.

"At least think about it," he begged again. She nodded.

They chatted briefly about other things, albeit slightly uncomfortably. He asked about her parents, and she about the department store, and how he was coping with the AA meetings. Neither mentioned Barry or Margot.

The next day, he sent an enormous bouquet of flowers to her at work, with a note saying, "To The Future…" Tears welled in her eyes, as she thought of what could have been. What should have been.

They started seeing each other a couple of times a week. Mitch tried to exert more pressure each time, and frequently asked to remarry her.

Diana finally decided to put him to the test. "If there is to be any kind of reconciliation, you will have to agree to counseling. It can be joint counseling if you like."

"But I'm already going to AA twice a week."

"That's the deal," Diana responded firmly. He reluctantly agreed. If that's what it took and if that's what made her happy, he would do it.

They continued counseling for six months, learning a lot about themselves and each other from their sessions. Diana learned forgiveness and was able to rid herself of the anger she had been carrying. Mitch unloaded the guilt he had been living with since the devastating evening.

As soon as they stopped the counseling sessions, Mitch proposed to Diana again. This time she accepted.

The night before the wedding, Mitch didn't know if he could get through it without a drink. What if Diana had cold feet and changed her mind? She had every right to. Could he go on without her now, having finally found her again and won her over? What if he had another lapse in being faithful? Could he go through all that guilt and suffering? Could he subject Diana to that pain again?

He lay on his bed in a tormented state, when the phone rang. It was Diana.

"I love you," she said quietly. "See you tomorrow afternoon."

It was the simple reassurance he needed from her. He confided in her his doubts and concern, but she calmed him. It was almost as if she sensed his nervousness and knew instinctively to call.

When he picked her up the next afternoon, he said sincerely, "You look as beautiful as you did the first day I met you," and hugged and kissed her tenderly.

"There's that charm again," she teased, as he closed her car door.

Mitch started the engine and steered the car in the direction of the Chapel of Eternal Love.

Chapter 17
Love Atop the Stratosphere

If your two favorite movies are *An Affair To Remember* and *Sleepless In Seattle*, mail me.

"That should do it. Let's see what happens," Julian said aloud to no one. He sat by the window looking at the Pacific Ocean from his beach front home on the island of Oahu. It was his first posting to any internet dating service.

Julian was an extremely handsome, masculine, young man in his mid twenties who had inherited the best traits of both his Hawaiian mother and Italian father. His jet black hair complemented an olive-skinned complexion and dark brown eyes. He had a cleft chin, baby dimples when he smiled, and a good, strong, physique developed over the years from surfing. Born and raised in Hawaii, he had never ventured off the islands. His parents owned one of the most successful orchid farms in the entire state of Hawaii as well as a pair of florist shops in Honolulu and Waikiki. Naturally, Julian, as the only son, had been part of the family business his entire life. He worked on the farm during school vacations, and was groomed to take over the family operation. Horticulture was part of his way of life, and being a nature lover, he reveled in being a major part of the lucrative enterprise that had already made him quite wealthy.

Hayley shook her umbrella before folding it away and entering her small apartment in Manhattan. It had been a busy day at the florist where she worked, and she was exhausted from having to fight her way home on the subway. As the rain poured down outside, she ran a hot bath where she could relax and rest her weary feet. She lit the candles around the bathtub, put on a soft background music CD, squeezed some drops from assorted aromatherapy essences into the water, and stepped slowly into the tub, prepared for a long soak. Later, wrapped in her warm dressing gown, she went to her desk to check the emails on her computer. There was nothing of interest, so she checked the internet dating service, to see if anything was new.

The brevity and nuances in Julian's posting was not lost on her. She knew instantly he was a true romantic, and she could not pass up the opportunity. She emailed him, equally brief. "Definitely, my two favorites. The original of *Affair*—not the remake," she added. She thought for a few moments and decided to offer a little more. "*Love Story, Gone With The Wind,* and *Dr. Zhivago* round out my top five." She was not about to elaborate, thinking her short response would be sufficient to let him know that she, too, was an incurable romantic, and hoped that her answer would create an element of intrigue.

Julian tapped into his email inbox, and was stunned by the number of responses he had received ... from all over the world. Diligently he looked at them all. None appealed to him, until he came across Hayley's email. She knew exactly what was behind his original internet posting, and he loved

The Chapel of Eternal Love

the movies she added. He responded straight away, giving a brief but honest description of himself and his life in Hawaii.

Just my luck, Hayley thought, seeing he lived in Hawaii. *I finally meet a romantic and he is G.U.*—her term for someone she considered geographically undesirable. It wasn't that she didn't want to visit Hawaii. She dreamed about going there. She hated the rat race of New York. It was so materialistic, and the men she dated were shallow yuppies in her eyes. She paused before responding to Julian, not sure if there was any future relationship. But something inside, perhaps her intuition, convinced her to pursue the correspondence. If nothing else, maybe she would have a good friend with whom she could email.

She wrote back describing her life in the Big Apple. She loved her job in the florist shop, but disliked the commute, the traffic congestion, and the fast pace of life. His tranquil life seemed idyllic by comparison.

"It is idyllic," Julian wrote back. "I am only missing someone to share my paradise with. I love strolling along the sandy beach watching the sun disappear, listening to the soft and gentle sounds of the surf as it rolls along the shore. I just need someone who enjoys the quiet, home life, and simple joys of nature."

Hayley was sold. It sounded like sheer heaven to her. She emailed him a photo of herself, and he responded in kind. Upon seeing his picture, Hayley was really smitten. She had wondered if he would be a bit of a geek and couldn't believe how handsome he really was.

Julian was equally struck with his good find. Hayley was petite, with a beautiful pixielike face, blond hair partially covering her left eye in front, and curling up around her neck. Her makeup was softly applied. He liked that. *What a knockout*, he thought as he looked at her trim, but shapely figure.

Before long, they started communicating by phone, which wasn't easy, given the time difference. Julian tried to call her every day at his lunch time, by which time Hayley would be home from work, and they talked endlessly every Sunday.

When it was finally time to meet, Julian had the perfect plan. "Why don't we meet half way? I'll pay your air fare and expenses," he insisted.

"Where do you suggest we meet?"

"In Las Vegas. We can meet in July, which will be exactly six months to the day since you first answered my posting. It is also my birthday weekend. There is a hotel called the Stratosphere, which has a revolving restaurant at the top. We can meet there. It will be just like Cary Grant and Deborah Kerr meeting on top of the Empire State building in New York. I'll make all the arrangements."

Hayley was not sure about meeting in Las Vegas in July, when the weather would be sweltering hot, but she loved the romance of it.

"Sounds fabulous," she said. "But we cannot meet each other beforehand. I'll find my way from the airport. Our first meeting will have to be at the restaurant."

"Done deal," said Julian.

"After all this time, I never knew you were a Cancer. I'm a Scorpio," she said, knowing what a good mix that was astrologically. That explained the good chemistry that was developing between them.

Julian booked separate rooms for them at the Stratosphere,

and arranged to fly to Las Vegas a day ahead to scout the city and make it the perfect romantic weekend. He packed a glass vase in his check-in baggage, and the day of his departure, arose early and picked some fresh orchids that he packed in a box to carry onto the plane. After landing at McCarran Airport, he picked up his rental car and drove straight to the hotel to check the rooms where they were staying. He unpacked his orchids and arranged them in the vase. He couldn't wait until the following evening. Hayley would soon be there.

The next day, he requested that the staff deliver the flowers to Hayley's room, which was adjacent to his. He attached a card saying, "From my heart." Then he visited most of the spots he anticipated taking Hayley to. It was all to be a surprise for her.

On the flight to Vegas, Hayley was full of excitement at meeting Julian and wondered what romantic escapades he had planned. She had been fantasizing about the weekend and meeting Julian since he had first proposed the idea. She hoped it would not be a big disappointment, and more importantly, that her dreams of her Prince Charming would not be shattered. She caught a cab to the hotel, and when she entered her room, was overwhelmed by the beautiful orchids that greeted her, and loved the sentimental card that accompanied it. She was of a mind to call Julian and thank him, but thought it would break the moment and detract from the excitement of their rendezvous later. Instead, she opted to take a nap before preparing herself for the evening.

Julian dressed in his best black slacks, dress shirt and burgundy-colored bow tie, and put on his white dinner jacket. The jacket contrasted sharply with his skin tone and accentuated his tanned, good looks. He caught the elevator to the lounge above the Top of The World Restaurant at a quarter to six, fifteen minutes before the appointed time. He wanted to make sure to be there before she arrived.

Precisely at six o clock, the elevator opened and Hayley stepped out. She looked stunning and seductive in a tight-fitting strapless black velvet dress that highlighted her platinum blond hair and emphasized her trim figure. Julian stared in awe. He was finally looking at the woman of his dreams.

She was equally impressed that Julian had dressed for the occasion. He moved toward her, his smile expressing his pleasure at what he was seeing and she saw his dimples for the first time. He looked so dapper, so cute and handsome ... so very handsome. What a moment.

His strong arms wrapped around her, as he first hugged her, then kissed her softly on the cheek, not wishing to overdo it at their first meeting. He escorted her to their dinner table and held back a chair for her to sit down. Being very genteel and feminine, she loved that gesture of old-fashioned manners. Julian beckoned the wine steward to open the bottle of chilled champagne in the wine bucket at the side of the table. He proposed a toast to Hayley, to a beautiful weekend, and to the future. It was a magnificent setting with the restaurant revolving so slowly, and the sun beginning to set. Hayley pinched herself to see if everything was real. She thanked him for his gorgeous orchids—and his card. He picked up her hand and caressed it.

As they enjoyed their dinner and champagne, they reveled in each other's company, thankful they were finally meeting after so many months of telephoning and emailing.

They looked out over the lights of the city, which looked like thousands of scattered jewels on a velvet carpet.

Stepping alone into the elevator after dinner, Hayley said dreamily, "This has to be the most wonderful evening of my entire life."

"Mine, too." Julian leaned over and kissed her on her lips. Hayley thought she was going to faint.

Julian accompanied Hayley to her room. "I know you must be tired from jetlag and the time difference," he said. "Why don't you sleep in tomorrow. I'll call you at nine-thirty."

Hayley nodded, although she was a little disappointed that the evening was coming to an end. Still, Julian was right, she was exhausted.

Nine-thirty sharp, Julian called. She felt rested and ready for a day of adventure with Julian. "Dress casual ... jeans," he told her. She wondered what he had lined up.

He drove her to their first port of call, the Venetian Hotel, and the gondola ride. Per Julian's prearranged request, the gondolier sang the theme song from *An Affair To Remember* in a rich baritone voice as he punted the gondola along the canal. Overcome with emotion, Hayley lay back with Julian's arms wrapped around her, tears welling in her eyes. He smiled down at her. They were both silent appreciating the tenderness of the moment. When the ride was over, they strolled through the canal shops, before enjoying a brunch style lunch upstairs at Zeffirino's Italian restaurant overlooking the canal.

Then, for a slight contrast and change of pace, Julian drove to Hoover Dam, and continued on to the west rim of the Grand Canyon. They liked the drive, the solitude, and knew they would be seeing one of the world's most magnificent and spectacular natural sights. As they watched the sun sinking behind the quiet rock structures, Julian had arranged for a late afternoon horseback ride along the rim of the canyon. It was a different world for both of them, especially for Hayley who only knew big city life. They sat and marveled at the spectacle before driving back to Las Vegas, with the sun roof wide open. Hayley saw the moon and the stars above. They were both strangely silent as they reflected on how they had thoroughly enjoyed their day and each other.

"I hope it isn't too much of an inconvenience, but can you have your bags packed and ready at six-thirty tomorrow morning?" Julian asked.

"Why? Where are we going?" Hayley wondered, somewhat mystified.

"You'll see," he said and kissed her goodnight.

Six-thirty Sunday morning, Hayley was ready.

"Oh Julian. How wonderful!" she exclaimed as they arrived for the hot air balloon ride. It took off toward Red Rock Canyon, just as the sun was rising, just the two of them. How wonderfully romantic, she thought. What a perfect start to the day. They were carefree and falling rapidly in love with each other. Everything was going just as Julian planned.

They returned to the hotel, and Julian checked them both out.

"Where are we headed now?" Hayley asked again.

"You'll see." He loved surprising her. "Right now, we're going to Sterlings. I understand it's the best champagne brunch in town."

They were seated in a quiet corner of the elegant restaurant, savoring the beautiful array of gourmet delights on display, accompanied by endless glasses of champagne. They were both relaxed and enjoying each other. Afterward, Julian took the short drive across the street to the doyenne of Las Vegas hotels, the Bellagio, and pulled up at the valet entrance.

"What are we doing here?" Hayley asked in disbelief.

"It's our last night in Las Vegas, and I want it to be special and memorable. I have booked us a mini-suite overlooking the fountains." He stopped for a minute and looked at Hayley. "I just reserved one room. I hope that's okay." She looked back at him and into his eyes, nodding.

They checked in and then went to explore the hotel. They visited the atrium, the art gallery, and beautiful shops, finally stopping at the little jewelry store in the hotel lobby. Hayley tried on a few rings admiringly. "It's like the movie *Breakfast At Tiffany's*," she laughed.

They returned to the room, both a little giddy from the effects of the champagne. It was late afternoon. They held hands and watched the fountain show outside their window. They turned and looked at each other. The moment was right. Julian put his arm around Hayley, picked her up, and slowly carried her into the bedroom. He laid her gently on the bed, and went to place the "Do Not Disturb" sign on the door.

Julian slowly undressed her, caressing her body all the while. She certainly had him aroused. Hayley was aching for Julian's touch and was ready to surrender her body to him. He was every bit as passionate as she had dreamed he would be. For Julian, she was the most tender and responsive lover. Their lovemaking was in unison as they explored each other's bodies. The flames of their souls seemed to ignite.

After their lovemaking, they lay quiet for a while.

Eventually, Julian headed to take a shower. Hayley waited until he finished, and then decided to enjoy a soak in the bath.

For the evening, Julian thought it would be nice if they had room service where they could have dinner alone while enjoying the fountain shows. They could be with each other. Besides, he knew neither of them would be that hungry after the sumptuous brunch.

Hayley was a little morose. It had been a perfect weekend, which was now coming to an end. But she was not about to let that deflate her last evening. She had found the man of her dreams. After finishing dinner, Hayley said excitedly, "I know, you thought I had forgotten it was your birthday. Well I haven't." She went to the bedroom, returning with a beautifully wrapped box.

Julian opened the gift and picked up the very classy looking watch. On the back were inscribed the words, "Anything is possible—Hayley." It was the partial line from his favorite movie *An Affair To Remember*.

Julian was truly touched at her thoughtfulness and generosity. He knew Hayley was the one to share his life. He knelt down in front of her and pulled a box out of his pocket. He looked up at her, and opened the box. "Will you marry me?" he asked.

Hayley gasped. Inside was the heart-shaped ring with small alternating diamonds and rubies she had tried on and admired earlier that day in the Bellagio jewelry store. He had run to the shop and purchased it while she was having her bath.

She threw her arms around him. "Oh, yes! Oh, yes! I'm the luckiest and happiest girl alive," she exclaimed ecstatically.

Julian was elated. He was not sure that he had won her over. Now he knew. He picked her up and carried her into the bedroom again.

With mixed emotions, they said their farewells the next day at McCarran Airport. They had found their true love, but it would be a while before they would see each other again.

Julian suggested that they get married in six months, the anniversary of when she first replied to his internet posting. It seemed an eternity, but he suggested that she fly to Hawaii for Thanksgiving to meet his parents, and he would travel to New York at Christmas to meet hers.

November was soon upon them, and as a birthday gift, he paid for her flight to Oahu. She loved his home on the beach. *A bit masculine*, she thought, observing the matching leather couch and loveseat and hardwood floors. A woman's touch would help. She observed the built-in bookcase in the living room, filled with a comprehensive collection of DVDs.

"I'm a homebody," Julian noted, as if reading her mind. "I am not a party animal or a night owl. I'm content to relax at night and watch movies. Especially since you'll be with me."

Hayley adored his parents. They were both so down to earth and hospitable. They made her feel part of the family immediately, welcoming her with open arms. She could see how Julian inherited his charm. It was a stark contrast to her family life.

She also fell in love with the island of Oahu. They went snorkeling, catamaran sailing and visited Waimea Falls, the pineapple fields, and of course, his orchid farm.

"Christmas will be a nightmare for you. There is so much hostility between my parents, they won't even be civil to each other on birthdays or holidays. I have to alternate. This year, we will do Christmas with Mother, and New Years with Father. That way you can meet them both," she said forlornly.

Christmas came soon enough, and Julian made his first trip to Manhattan. It was cold and damp. They skated at the Rockefeller Center, went to the Statue of Liberty, took a carriage ride in Central park, and of course, visited the Empire State building. They were so in love. He enjoyed meeting both her parents, though he did find them a little aloof.

Julian suggested that they meet in Las Vegas, and get married at a chapel there. "Afterward we can have dinner atop the Stratosphere, where we first met," he said exuberantly. "I've located a chapel called The Chapel Of Eternal Love. It's perfect, since that's what I'm offering you—my eternal love."

"It *is* perfect. It's a perfect plan," Hayley enthused.

They met again in Las Vegas. He arrived early and checked into the Bellagio before heading back to the airport to meet Hayley. He wanted to ensure that everything was in order. They both freshened up and changed for the ceremony. Before they left the hotel, they stopped at the same jewelry store where he purchased her engagement ring, so they could select wedding rings.

They drove to the chapel, having booked the last appointment of the day. As soon as the ceremony was finished, they needed to be at the Top of the World restaurant at six o'clock.

Buster greeted the car, barking loudly and wagging his tail

feverishly. Rosemary couldn't quiet him down. She recognized that wag as well as the tone of the bark. This was going to be one happy, happy marriage.

As they stood at the altar, Julian had a wedding surprise for her. Rosemary sat down at the piano and began playing one of her most frequently requested songs. On hand was the gondolier who had serenaded them at the canal six months earlier, in his rich baritone voice, singing the theme song of *An Affair To Remember.*

Chapter 18

A Day in the Life
of a Wedding Chapel

As the sun set on the Las Vegas skyline, the lights on the plush hotels and casinos began to sparkle. It was the time when the marquees and billboards came to life.

Rosemary chatted briefly with the mailman delivering the letters to her office.

"My, you're late today," she commented.

"Don't know why. It's just been one of those days," he said.

Indeed it was, Rosemary agreed. For her it was just another day in the life of a Las Vegas wedding chapel.

She watched the cleaning crew exit the van with their mops and buckets and head toward the chapel. She waved at them as she opened the mail and wrote checks for the bills that had come in. It was her custom. She hated there to be any unpaid bills at the end of the day. She wrote the bank deposit, which she always dropped in the night box on her way to work the following morning. She felt safer doing it then, when it was light, as opposed to the darkness she encountered when driving home.

"Good night, Rosemary," the minister yelled from his office as left. "Don't forget to lock up."

It irritated her that he said it every night, as if it was something she would forget to do. She switched off the coffee machine, rinsed the pot and coffee cup so they would be ready for the next day, and flicked on the flashing neon light: "chapel closed."

She locked the office door and headed through the back door toward the chapel, bolting the rear entrance door behind her. She briefly inspected the floors to ensure that the cleaning crew had done its job thoroughly and touched the seats to see if there was any dust. She was only too aware that many of the chapels in Las Vegas were sometimes dirty. Her chapel was a cut above all the others. She took pride in it. *The roses could last a few more days*, she thought, as she poured more water into the large vase.

She sat, as she did every night, in the front pew for a few moments, with Buster curling up at her feet. It was her favorite time of day. She embraced the quiet and solitude the chapel invoked, and liked to reflect on the ceremonies that had taken place during the day.

She thought of her old school chum, Pru, and her gigolo boyfriend. She still had her doubts on that marriage. Then she thought of poor Rosa, the illegal immigrant and a startling revelation occurred to her. *Of course! Why didn't I think of it sooner? Rosa could work at one of Pru's hotels. I'm sure Pru could help Rosa with her legal problem,* she thought. Rosa would at least get a decent paycheck and would finally be able to bring her husband to America for his operation. She would call Pru the next day. She felt better about that situation already.

Suddenly, Buster rose from his spot and trotted to the chapel entrance. Rosemary thought nothing of it. She did not hear the footsteps of anyone entering the chapel. She heard Buster whining joyfully as she turned around to see an elderly man standing at the chapel entrance, Buster leaping up at his side. She jumped.

"You startled me, Sir."

"I'm sorry. I didn't mean to," he said.

The man was somewhere in his seventies, Rosemary thought. Even so, he was quite good looking with silver hair around the sides of his bald head. He appeared lost as he surveyed the chapel. He touched the wooden pews and seemed to be marveling at them. She could see his eyes glistening as he looked around at the mosaic glass windows. "Quite incredible! Magnificent!" he said in awe.

"I'm sorry, Sir. The chapel is now closed. But if there is anything I can help you with, we'll be open tomorrow."

"Oh, I'll only be a few minutes," he said as he walked toward her. "I'm on my way to a Christian retreat in California. I have to be there tomorrow afternoon. You see, I built this chapel fifty years ago, and I couldn't pass through Las Vegas without stopping to see if it was still here. I thought it might have given way to a freeway or a high-rise building or a new hotel. This is the first time I have been back to Las Vegas since I left all those years ago."

"Oh, you must be Pastor Glen!" She rose from her seat, somewhat astonished. She was totally familiar with the history and origins of the chapel. "My name is Rosemary. I am so honored to meet you. I can't believe it," she gushed, extending her hand.

"Please, don't get up." The pastor motioned her to sit. He sat down in the pew across the aisle from her. He continued looking around the chapel as if absorbing all the minute details. "It seems like time has stood still. It's almost as if I never left," he confided.

"Well, the piano could use a bit of a tune-up, I suppose," Rosemary offered a little sheepishly.

"And how long have you been here?" He seemed genuinely interested.

"Oh, it's been just on twenty years now. The minister has been here just over three years. What a pity, you just missed him. Perhaps you could come by tomorrow morning before you leave for California. He'd love to meet you, I'm sure."

"I'd like that. I'd like to see the chapel during the daytime, too."

He seemed quite impressed Rosemary had worked at the chapel for such a long time. "Unbelievable. Fancy you have worked here for twenty years. How many weddings have you witnessed?"

"Oh, hundreds! Thousands!" she laughed.

"I wonder how many of the weddings have lasted?" pondered the pastor.

"Judging from the Christmas cards I receive every year, a large number of them. I've been receiving cards from some of the couples since I first came here. Why, even today, I had two couples renewing their vows who married here twenty-five years ago. Their children were married today as well. Of course, it was an Elvis wedding," she chuckled. "But they still took their vows seriously. We even had a couple this afternoon who had divorced and were remarrying!"

"Amazing! And do you get all religions here? I always hoped the chapel would be non-denominational."

"Oh yes. This morning we had a young Catholic marrying a Jewish lady. They were so much in love. The nice thing is, Pastor Glen, we get people of all ages, too. The day began with a couple who were in their twenties … motorcycle fanatics they were. They were followed by a couple who had to be in their late seventies. We had another couple marrying late in life. I think she was a lady of the night, as they say," she shared. "But there is no doubt in my mind, she and her husband will be happy. Yes, we get them all here."

The Pastor was spellbound. Rosemary could see he was listening intently to what she was saying.

"We even had a soldier serving in Iraq marrying," she continued. "And an army veteran who reunited with his former Vietnamese girlfriend."

"This is all so wonderful," Pastor Glen marveled. "I never knew the chapel would have such weddings. From what I read in the papers I thought that Las Vegas chapels just have celebrity drop-in weddings and what have you."

"Well, we get those, too, from time to time." She sniffed her wrist, to see if the perfume given her by Peter and Renee was still as fragrant. "And we do have our share of unusual ceremonies. Today we had two sets of twins marrying each other. They looked so cute. We even had a couple who came with their little daughter. I am not sure what their story was, but they certainly were in love." Then she thought of poor Emmy. "Unfortunately, we have the occasional ceremony where either the bride or groom gets cold feet at the last minute and one of them is left standing at the altar. That's always tough." She became pensive, as she wondered what the future held for Emmy.

Pastor Glen shook his head. "Well, marriage isn't for everyone, I guess. Did you never find the love of your life?"

"Why, Pastor Glen. The chapel *is* the love of my life." She gestured around the chapel. "At the end of the day, I feel all the love emanating from the walls of this building—from all the couples who have been married here. The last young couple here today, a young Hawaiian man and his wife, were so in love it was unbelievable. I am a part of their happiness—their true happiness."

Pastor Glen's eyes glistened again. For years he had struggled with Laura's passing and questioned why. Now he finally realized that her short life had meaning. It was not in vain. Her life and love lived on through the chapel ... the chapel he had built in her memory. He could feel her spirit and presence all around him. He knew she was beaming.

"I would so love to hear more of your experiences at the chapel, yet I have so little time. Would it be an imposition if I asked you to have dinner with me this evening?"

Rosemary thought for a moment. She realized how much it would mean to him if she indulged his curiosity. Besides, much of her own happiness was because of his building the chapel. Who knows where her life might have gone had she not signed on all those years ago. She hesitated. Then she nodded and smiled. "I'd be delighted to."

She suddenly remembered she had invited Derek and Jenny over to her home if things didn't work out with their parents. She was almost certain that once they recovered from the shock, the parents would show some understanding about Jenny's pregnancy, and even if they didn't, she was doubtful Jenny and Derek would arrive at her doorstep. But Rosemary had made the commitment, and her sense of duty dictated that she honor it.

"I'm sorry. I just realized I do need to be at home this evening." She saw no reason to go into the details with the pastor.

He looked crestfallen at the sudden change of plans. Rosemary felt bad, as it was clearly important to him to learn more about the chapel.

"I'll tell you what. If you don't mind something plain and simple, I could rustle us up something at my place. I'm not a fancy cook, but I can throw together some spaghetti and a salad, if you like. I only live ten minutes from here."

"Oh, I'd hate to impose. That would be putting you to too much trouble."

"Not at all," Rosemary chided. "I'd be delighted."

She got up from her seat. Pastor Glen stood up and offered his arm. She linked her arm in his and they walked to the entrance of the chapel. "Come along, Buster," she called. She heard the pitter patter of his feet following behind them.

She switched off the lights, locked the chapel door behind her, and they walked down the few steps and across the small car park together, chatting incessantly.

Buster trotted behind them panting slightly, his tail wagging.

About the Author

Stephen Murray was born in England and raised in the Southern Africa region. Upon completion of his high school education, he returned to England before moving to California in 1976. He has travelled extensively throughout the world. Stephen owns a computer software company. Apart from travelling and writing, he enjoys theatre, concerts, music, reading and current affairs. He makes his home in Las Vegas, Nevada, where he has lived since May 2003.

For questions, comments, or to order additional copies of this book, please visit **www.thechapelofeternallove.com**, email him at stephen@casandras.net, or write to:

Casandras
9811 W. Charleston Blvd., Ste. 2-354
Las Vegas, NV 89117